THE XMAS DAY BUTCHER

A 25-Day Christmas Advent Thriller
Written by Spencer Guerrero

Table of Contents

Content Warnings

POTENTIAL SPOILERS BELOW

This book includes death, murder, abduction, depiction of severe mental illness, severed human limbs, and some graphic scenes of violence.

Reader Discretion Is Advised.

If you have any questions or concerns about the content/trigger warnings in this book—please feel more than free to email it to me:
info@spencerguerreroauthor.com
I want to ensure that you have a great reading experience!

25 DAYS...

You may read this Christmas Advent Thriller—1 chapter a day—until Christmas Day. Join THE SUS-PENCERS Group on Facebook to join in on the fun and the daily discussion posts!

OR

You may it read it all, as you please.

ENJOY THE SHOW...

"We all have a hidden monster lurking within us."

— *S.G.*

CHAPTER 1
DECEMBER 1ST

Whisper's Creek always had this haunted stillness to it, like the town was trying its best to stay alive, but it continued to decay and degrade, all the same. Like a hidden darkness was trying to drag it down to the depths of hell.

My wife, Angela, bless her kind heart, was doing her best to save it. She worked with Mayor Hamonte and wanted to restore Whisper's Creek to something respectable—a place that you'd actually want to live in.

The joyous month of December had finally commenced, so that meant that Christmas decorations hung from every lamp post and window throughout the town square and shopping centers. I took it all in as I traveled through the outdoor plaza; I had planned on doing some gift shopping for Christmas.

The decorations reminded me of how dark the town had become, because Christmas was the only time when the town felt a sense of peace and light. Throughout the year, it was like someone pressed pause on a place that should've been growing, improving, and getting better, but now, we all just quietly accepted our doomed fates.

I wanted to move far, far away and never return—never looking back on the dark, depraved town of Whisper's Creek—but Angela wouldn't have it. She was one of those people who liked to save things, to take matters into her own hands—the type of wonderful woman who uplifted the poor and innocent souls of the world.

I didn't have the heart to tell her that I wanted to get the heck out of Whisper's Creek. I told myself that as long as I was with her, I'd be okay. I'd live. So, I kept my hidden desires to myself.

What a goddamn mistake that turned out to be.

I tried to enjoy the tinsel, the red and green lights, and the holiday cheer as best I could. Christmas hadn't meant much to me since... well, I didn't like to think about it. Even in my 30s, revisiting those violent memories felt like I was stabbing myself in the heart with a jagged knife. In truth, Christmas hadn't meant much to me for a long time.

But Angela? She loved it. The joy, the decorating, the same songs that blared from all the retail shops in town. I did my best to play along for her. She deserved it. What happened to me so long ago was not her fault; I didn't need to punish her for it.

I stepped into a corner shop just as the doorbell chimed softly, bringing some swirling snowflakes alongside with me.

"Hello, Merry Christmas!" an elderly man shouted. "Merry Christmas, young man!" I replied back, and I was met with his appreciative laughter. It was a jolly period of time and I did my best to play the part.

The shop smelled like a mix of cinnamon and pumpkin-scented candles. Fake snowflakes hung from the ceiling, colorful Christmas ornaments lined the shelves, and mechanical Santas twerked around in the front section of the store—behind the display glass.

My eyes immediately spotted the glass case where the bracelets were displayed. The one I'd been thinking about for weeks was right there, sparkling in the yellow light.

It was a long silver chain, with five small golden rings clasped to it. Angela loved things with meaning, things that were thoughtful. Five years was how many years we'd been married. How time flew when you tied the knot to the sweetheart of your dreams.

I went over to check out the silver chain when I heard a familiar voice behind me.

"Is that *the* Lenny? What's up, little man?"

I turned and saw Joseph Candela, standing near the back of the store. He was a big, burly man wrapped in a black fur coat, holding a twerking Santa. I noticed that his rosy cheeks were bright red because of the cold. It made him look like a young Santa Claus.

"Hello Joseph," I said, glancing at him. "It's nice to see you."

He inspected the twerking Santa further, his large dark eyes lighting up as it danced. Joseph was always a strange fellow. I couldn't tell if he was just trying to be funny or if he was hiding something.

"Can you believe this wonderful Christmas technology? I know I'm the target audience for sure," he said, referring to the Santa toy, laughing heartily at it. "So, my friend, are you buying something for Angela?" he asked as he set down the twerking Santa and walked towards me.

"Yes, I am." I nodded, tapping on the glass where the jewelry was. "Something she really wanted. She's not that hard to shop for. She gives me hints."

Angela made everything easy for me, and I always appreciated that about her.

Joseph gave a low whistle. "That's one hell of a gift, man. Not every guy exerts that much effort or dollar bills. But Angela...oh man, she deserves it. I know what you're doing." He winked at me.

I don't understand why Joseph has to say things like that—like he wants to sleep with my wife. I don't appreciate it.

I shrugged, indifferent to his weird tone. "You're right, she does deserve it."

There was an awkward pause before Joseph continued, "Angela's a pretty lady. Those beautiful eyes and that long, soft hair. Such a hard worker too. You're a lucky little shit." He noticed my silence and lightly bumped my shoulder. "Just messing with you, man, I'm keeping you on your toes."

I let out a dry chuckle. "What can I say? She's one of the best things that has ever happened to me. In a lot of ways—she saved me."

He got closer to me, deciding to examine a plush elf on a rack beside us. "I know that you'll always appreciate her. Because I know that the day you don't, she'll probably leave and find something better. There's always someone waiting for that to happen."

I looked at him quietly as he stared back at me—his expression was stone-like, and I wasn't sure what he was trying to accomplish here.

What message was he trying to convey to me? That he was going to steal her from me?

"I'll always appreciate her, you don't have to worry about that—*my friend*," I replied icily, refusing to break eye contact with him.

Joseph's stony face broke into a smile as he patted me on the back a bit too aggressively. "I'm just messing with ya! You know that, right? I'm just the jokester, man. We're all good."

I looked away from him, anger inflating my chest. "Right, I know that. You're just full of jokes, aren't you?"

"That I am. Around the holidays I get jollier too."

I paused for a second, contemplating on whether or not I should say it, to save my dignity. "And full of yourself," I ended up saying.

His eyes locked onto mine, his face turning sour. I waited for his smart-ass reply.

He smiled and laughed. "That's a good one, Lenny!" He fist-bumped me and then walked to the front of the store. "Happy Holidays, man! Good luck with Angela and that gift!" he pushed open the door and left.

"Yeah, you too, Joseph," I quietly said through gritted teeth. I barely considered him a friend, but I tolerated him because there weren't many people who lived in Whisper's Creek to begin with. He also worked with Angela in the mayor's office. He was a maintenance man. I was sure he stared at her any chance he got. It made my blood boil.

I watched him walk out of the shop from the window, his shoulders hunched against the sharp, cold winds. Part of me wanted to brush off his strange commentary, and I told myself it was harmless. But I couldn't shake the feeling I had in the pit of my stomach. What he said still didn't sit right with me, no matter how hard I tried to set it aside. It still lingered in my mind, dark possibilities echoing around my head.

I didn't like the idea that he thought about her in ways he shouldn't have. I was sure that he wanted her all to himself, the secret sicko.

I picked up the chain and paid for it, eager to be on my way. The winds seemed to be picking up, and I still had a bit of a long way to go before I'd be home. The town was beginning to look like a white blur, the snowfall thickening by the second.

I cut across the town square, the sound of the wind howling in my ears. As I trudged through the rising snow, crunching through ice with each step, I couldn't help but glance at the shop windows—glowy, blinking lights reflecting off the glass, all those colors that were synonymous with the Christmas holiday.

Something rose in my throat, a dry lump that made tears fall from my eyes. It was hard for me during this time of year. It reminded me of what had happened—something that'd haunt me for the rest of my life.

I shook my head, trying to forget about what had happened. I'd rather focus on the future and the happiness I could still one day attain.

Once I reached the outskirts of the town square, there wasn't much for miles—just a bunch of snowy fields, trees, and the occasional farmhouse. Most of them were abandoned. I worked in one that wasn't.

Eventually, I crossed paths with my employer. There was George St. Nicklaus sitting on his front porch, outside his little farmhouse, his bulk blocking the door. He was hard to miss, like a living, breathing Santa Claus clone—red-faced, round as a caramel apple, and always coincidentally wearing winter attire that included color palettes of red, green, and white. His thick white beard always made me think of a worn-out Santa, minus the jolly part. I called him "Grumpy Claus" behind his back, of course. Although the man had a temper and had trust issues, he trusted me with a key to the farmhouse.

"Lenny!" he boomed, spotting me from across the street. "Did you get that ham I told you about?"

I forced a grateful smile. "Yeah, I got it, George."

He grunted, his beady eyes nervously scanning across the snowy land. "Good. That's the only thing that makes this damn season worth my time. You can never beat my Christmas ham. Clara used to love it and always devoured it. I make the best damn Christmas ham in this godforsaken town!"

I had no idea why he had such a fascination with ham, but so be it. Everyone needed something to fixate on in life. I fixated on how much I hated living in Whisper's Creek, but in secret. Angela was the only light in my life, and I never wanted to upset her—part of the reason I was buying her the chain.

Clara was George's daughter. She went missing about a year ago, creepily vanished without a trace, though George is convinced someone killed her. That's when the trouble began—when Clara disappeared into thin air.

He stood up, shaking his candy cane at me. "By the way, come by to fix those bathroom cabinets. I don't like seeing them open when I'm trying to squeeze the excrement out of my—"

"I'll handle it! I got it—don't you worry, sir." I nodded politely, feeling the weight of his angry eyes on me as I turned to leave.

George was one of those bitter old men who had no one left in life—no one left to love or yell at. Those were his words, not mine.

But underneath that grumpy attitude, he had a softness when it came to Clara. He did love his only daughter, maybe a little too much—according to the townsfolk. From what I observed when she was still around, he liked to control her and frequently told her what to do. She didn't like that. She was 22 years old, and she liked to do as she pleased. I never meddled in those affairs, but I often wondered what might've happened to little Clara St. Nicklaus.

With a quick, respectful nod to Grumpy Claus, I marched on, wrapping my reindeer-themed coat tighter around my chest against the freezing winds that had picked up. I wasn't far from home now.

It was a hard town to love, Whisper's Creek. Angela had always been able to find the simple beauty in it. It was one of the things I admired most about her, the way she could see hope in places where it seemed like it had died a long time ago.

When my home was in view and when some of the snowfall had subsided, that's when I saw it.

There was a dark shape on the porch of our house. At first, I thought it was just a pile of snow that had somehow accumulated or some delivery box from the post office.

When I got closer, the knot that had already been growing in my stomach tightened. I immediately knew that something was wrong, that something terrible had happened. I didn't know how I had it, but my gut knew—it always knew.

When I slowly came up the steps on the porch, I saw that it was a small gift box.

My heart dropped. I hadn't seen anyone leave it there, and I knew Angela hadn't been outside. I set the plastic bag I was holding down on the porch and crouched beside the gift box sealed with Christmas tape. My gloved hands were shaking as I carefully opened it.

Inside, there was a red envelope. I used my finger to rip it open, and inside was a white letter written in strange, scribbled handwriting. The paper was perfectly white, in mint condition. I realized quickly that someone was meticulously toying with me and sending me a message that I needed to pay very close attention to.

CLUE #1: *"You have 24 days to find Angela. Your deadline is Christmas Day. Now, you must play my game. You only have yourself to blame. My life has been filled with strife; now find your missing wife. Signed, The Xmas Day Butcher."*

As my eyes analyzed the words, they didn't make any sense to me. I felt my breath escaping me, my heart pounding in my chest, my

vision blurring, and my mind racing to make sense of the madness
I had just read. I looked inside the box and searched inside to see if
there was anything else...there was.

A small, bloodstained object wrapped in tissue paper. My stomach
churned as I lifted it up.

A pair of reindeer earrings. These weren't just any earrings. Angela
wore those earrings; they belonged to her. The metal was tainted with
something dark and wet.

Someone had taken my beloved wife—a sick, deranged bastard.

A pained sob broke out of me as intense panic crawled up my
throat.

*No, this can't be real. This has to be some sick prank, some cruel joke
that Angela is playing on me. But she'd never do anything like this.
What the hell is going on? What have we done to deserve this?*

I stood up shakily—legs trembling—the gravity of the situation
was enveloping me whole. I had no idea what I was going to do.

The snowfall worsened around me, the bitter winds slicing my
cheeks, and my hands became numb as I stumbled backwards, losing
my balance. The cold air swiped the letter out of my hands and into
the darkness as the sunlight faded over Whisper's Creek.

I did the only thing I could think of in the moment: I screamed her
name like a wild beast that lived in the forest behind our house.

"Angela!" I shouted, my voice shrieking, her name echoing
through the dark, calm sky, hoping I'd reach her somehow—some
way.

I stared at the front door of our small house and bolted through it, my heart racing as I searched every room. I looked in the kitchen, the living room, and the bathroom. They were all empty. There was no sign or trace of her. She really had been taken.

As I doubled back, I found her fuzzy pink slippers on the floor of the kitchen, and her matching Christmas sweater with reindeer was draped over the back of the couch in the living room.

It seemed like she was immediately taken just as she got home. Like she didn't get the chance to really settle in. I thought of the back door and ran over to it; it was unlocked. I practically threw myself into it and busted it wide open, but I was met with rows and rows of snowy trees and white nothingness.

"Angela!" I screamed into the sky, my voice lost in the harsh gusts of wind.

There was no answer, not a single trace of human life in any direction from our home. The nearest neighbor was a few miles away. We lived in seclusion, and I had no idea who'd want to take my dear Angela away from me.

I dropped down to my knees and faced the cruel silence of the darkest night of my life. I got back up, slowly—preparing to face the fury of the coming storm. I marched into the cold, fully intent on retrieving the letter that said **CLUE #1**.

This Christmas Day changed my life forever.

CHAPTER 2
DECEMBER 2ND

I was standing at the top of the stairs, my small fingers tightly wrapped around the iron railing, while I stared down into a decorative living room. It was Christmas Day.

Golden tinsel clung to the white leather couch, and the fireplace quietly crackled as a family gathered around a Christmas tree adorned with various ornaments—from tiny snow globes to crystallized balls and candy canes.

There was a man and a woman—husband and wife. Their faces were wrinkled and hard, like a pair of stone golems turned human. They were cuddling on the couch, laughing and giggling with each other like schoolchildren.

A boy sat cross-legged in his raggedy pajamas, faded Santa hats printed along the fabric. He looked about twelve years old.

The resemblance was uncanny, then I realized who it was. I was staring at myself. Same cut of dark, wavy hair, same milky white skin, and that same scowling face I had because I hated the world and how I had to live in it.

The only difference now was that I had some spotty facial hair, and I had Angela to make living bearable.

"Where's my gift? Don't I get one?" the boy asked, an undercurrent of anger present in his innocent voice.

The man grunted, reaching for a bottle of alcohol on a side table. The woman giggled at him and wagged her finger at him, like she was indicating he had done something very wrong.

"No, this can't be right. Where's my present?" the boy shouted louder. "You said I'd get the doll! You told me that! You're both liars!"

There was a charged silence. Enraged with the boy, the man took a swig of the bottle and then smashed it on the floor. The woman's laughing abruptly ended, and she stared down, eyes darting over all of the broken shards of glass on the floor.

"You will stop your disrespect this instant!" the man shouted. "Or you'll face the consequences," he warned, lowering his intense gaze, beaming at him with fiery eyes.

"Stop your disrespect! Stop your whining!" she echoed.

The boy jumped up and balled his hands into tight fists. "I want the doll! Give me the doll!" he screamed, as his reddened face sagged into tears and subdued rage.

I had a nauseous feeling at the pit of my stomach. I wanted to rush down to stop him, to calm him down—before he made things worse. But my legs were stuck in place, and I couldn't move a muscle. I was only able to watch in horror from behind the railing as the chaotic scene unraveled—a memory I'd seen before. It was a recurring nightmare that lingered in my mind, half-asleep, half-awake, ready to torment me whenever I closed my eyelids.

Suddenly, from the corner of the room, a dark figure in a red coat and a plastic Santa mask darted toward the Christmas tree. My throat went dry as I stopped breathing. The demonic intruder yanked the star from the top of the tree—a long, pointed ornament, as sharp as a knife's blade—and turned to the squabbling family.

The man barely had time to look up as the intruder slashed his throat with the yellow star, a fountain of blood instantly pouring out all over him. A wave of panicked screaming and shouting bounced off the walls.

My legs became weak, and I collapsed to the ground, my eyes wide with shock—unable to look away from the gruesome violence that was unfolding in front of me. It was like being in the backseat of a speeding car, knowing you were about to crash into a brick wall and be pulverized into dust.

The woman's laughter had snuffed out as she gaped at the intruder, unable to make a sound, only quiet, breathy gasps—she knew what was coming to her.

The intruder viciously swiped at her throat, her final words nothing more than a gurgling noise as blood poured out of her—an instant, violent death.

The boy's screams shattered the air, high-pitched like an animal in pain, until suddenly—nothing. I squeezed my eyes shut and didn't dare look at the bloodied, chaotic mess that had exploded down below. I couldn't face it; I refused to.

When I heard loud stomps coming up the stairs—I jolted awake, my heart hammering in my chest, my hair slick with sweat, candy cane-themed sheets thrown on the floor...it had been a dream—no, a nightmare.

My bedroom was pitch black except for the faint orange glow of the rising sun peeking through a crack in the closed curtains. My icy skin was slick with cold sweat, and I tried my best to control my breathing.

It was a nightmare, just a nightmare. But...it happened. Maybe not like that...but it happened.

For a short moment I couldn't remember why I felt a knot in my stomach, like something had gone very wrong. Then it hit me—Angela. She was gone. She had been abducted by someone who called themselves the Xmas Day Butcher.

Oh no...Angela, my sweet Angela.

I tried to remember...when was the last time I had spoken with her? I slid out of bed slowly, raising my hand to the back of my head—it was pounding. I shut my eyes and tried to recall what had happened, or what could've happened. It all still felt like a fever dream—a gift box with a "clue" and a letter from someone named "The Xmas Day Butcher."

Seriously, what the hell was that all about?

I had seen her yesterday, in the morning. She had gone to work at the mayor's office, like she did every weekday. She worked for Mayor Carl Hamonte. He was divorced and had one son—Henry Hamonte—but his son had tragically died of alcohol poisoning last December. Not long after Clara had gone missing.

Angela was telling me about the restoration project she wanted to implement for Whisper's Creek.

I gave her a tight hug in the kitchen of our house and a quick kiss on the cheek, and off she went. After that, I went to go check on Grumpy Claus and did some menial chores for him. I texted her that I'd be home later because I went to buy her a Christmas gift; she hadn't replied. She never did end up replying, because this monster abducted her, and when I came home, I realized I was being forced to play some sick, twisted game.

What the hell am I supposed to do next?

A harsh sound broke up my quiet flurry of thoughts—two deliberate knocks pounded against the front door. I froze. Then there was another knock—louder and seemingly angrier.

Oh my—Angela? Can it be?

I rushed out of my bed, stumbling on the ice-cold floor, and pulled on a Santa Claus sweater that was hanging from my dresser near my door. I yanked open my drawer and quickly slipped on some Christmas Elf pajama pants and slid into my snowman slippers.

I left my room and quickly maneuvered my way through the darkened hallway while my heart raced, hoping it was Angela at the door and that everything would be okay after all.

It was a silly prank—just some dumb, silly prank.

When I got to the door and pulled it open, a blast of frigid air slapped my groggy face. To my surprise, it was Detective Juana Castillo who stood on the porch, her short, dark bob cut of hair littered with particles of snow. She was a strong, fit woman with the tattoo of a black spiral on her collarbone. I always wondered what that was about. Perhaps something to do with a cycle?

I liked to say she was as tough as hardwood itself. She was as strict and rigid as the ice that formed on the roof of my house.

She looked at me coldly, not saying a word, but in her gloved hands was a small gift box, sealed with Christmas-themed tape. Scrawled across the lid in red marker: **CLUE #2.**

My goodness, another damn box.

"Hello, Mr. Frost. This was left at the police station for you," she said stiffly, her voice low and serious. "There's no return address, and I don't know who left it."

I gently took it from her hands and stared at it, terrified at what was hidden inside.

My fingers trembled as I tore the tape to open it. "I know who left it." Inside, cushioned by crumpled packing paper, was a single ornament—a delicate, white Christmas ball streaked with dried blood.

Beneath it, a red envelope. I ripped it open with my finger. Inside was another white letter. I carefully slid it out, my breath frosting over in the cold as I hesitated to read what it said.

"Remember what you've done. There's nowhere for you to run."

CHAPTER 3
DECEMBER 3RD

B efore I could say much of anything to her, Detective Castillo had been called back to the police station because of an emergency—some road blockage caused by slippery, snow-covered streets that turned things really ugly near the roads that led out of town. That was the curse of Whisper's Creek at work. That's what I believed anyway.

I had brought in the second gift box with me, wondering what it all meant, my mind spinning in a million different directions.

"*Remember what you've done. There's nowhere for you to run.*"

What had I done? I didn't understand what the Xmas Day Butcher was trying to spell out to me—it didn't make any sense. I sat down in my white lounge chair, a drink in hand. I started downing it, not having a care in the world about what happened to me.

Suddenly, I heard a familiar voice: "*Don't call them, Lenny. Don't call them!*"

My mind started to go blank. Seconds turned to minutes, and minutes turned to hours as I slowly shut my eyes, longing for my wife's return, hoping she was alright—wherever she was.

A streak of sunlight washed over my closed eyelids causing me to pounce awake. I quickly checked my watch: **December 3rd**. I swallowed down the dryness in my sore throat and reached down for a water bottle that wasn't there—it was the bottle I had finished the day before. I didn't even remember passing out.

I didn't think Detective Castillo had returned because I didn't hear any knocking, nor did I hear my phone going off—that would've been George's incessant calling. He hated being ignored.

That's how my grief had begun to manifest—like a slow, seeping poison that infected my veins, my heart...and everything else that pulsated in my body. Not having Angela near me, safe with me...was taking its toll. I hadn't told the police yet because I didn't trust them, not the skeleton crew in Whisper's Creek anyway.

There was always something about them not having enough resources to do *anything* in the damn town; that's why Angela was trying to fix things any way she could. She was a good, kind soul that deserved all she wanted in the world—even if it refused to give it to her.

The police never even found George's daughter, Clara. She'd been missing since last year. Eventually, I knew that I'd have to rise up, out of my despair and hopelessness, to find Angela before it was too late.

The tragic event of her abduction had ignited something terrible in me, a feeling that I couldn't do anything to save anyone because of what had happened to me when I was a child. I had to push through it for Angela.

As if on cue, there was a hard knocking at the door. I quickly jumped up and rushed to open it. Detective Castillo was there, standing like a statue of ice.

"Hello again. May I come in?" I nodded and stepped aside.

Detective Castillo entered and shut the door behind her with a heavy thud that made the windows shake. She stood inside my living room, her black boots dripping melted snow onto the rug that had a Christmas tree design on it.

If Angela were here, she'd be very upset about stains on the rug.

The gift box with **CLUE #2** rested on a coffee table near the front door, like evidence of a murder.

"Tell me again," she said, arms crossed, her cold, dark eyes staring me down. "Why do you think you received this gift? What's going on here? You sounded very frantic on the phone, and I didn't understand you. You were telling me about some Xmas Day Butcher? A gift box you received? Sorry, I was dealing with something—severe road blockage near the institute. It's bad."

On the phone? What phone? Did I call her...oh god, I don't remember.

"I—I don't know. This is the second gift I've received." My voice sounded nervous and panicky, even as I was trying to stay calm. "I swear, I have no idea who would send it. I don't know what this is about."

"Really?" she tilted her head. "Because that letter implies that you've done something very wrong."

I swallowed hard. The ominous saying flashed in my mind: "Remember what you've done. There's nowhere for you to run."

But I haven't done anything. Have I? No, I'd never do anything to hurt anyone. Right?

I held up a finger, indicating for her to wait. I rushed back to my bedroom, grabbed the first gift box from underneath my bed, and ran back to the living room. I slowly handed it to her.

She took it from me gently, taking out the letter and examining it, her eyes reading the words of warning that were scribbled on it. She glanced up at me, her eyebrows furrowed, her mouth slightly agape. "What the hell is this?" she asked breathlessly, concern apparent in her tone of voice.

I paced back and forth while nervously rubbing my head, unsure of what to say. I only looked at her as she examined the bloodied reindeer earrings with shocked eyes, not daring to touch them.

I pointed at the box, waiting for her eyes to meet mine. "Those...those are Angela's. They belonged to her. Whoever this person is...they took her. They abducted my wife."

Detective Castillo stared at the floor for a moment before slowly placing the gift box on the coffee table beside her. "Wait... Angela is missing? Is that what you're saying?"

"I'm innocent, I swear it!" I sputtered, the words spilling out of my mouth like a sudden confession.

She slowly turned to me, hand on her holster. "What are you referring to, sir?" she asked carefully.

I swung my hands up in the air to show her I wasn't going to do anything crazy. "Detective...I haven't been absolutely truthful. Here's the thing—my wife is missing—Angela. I came home on December 1st, and she was gone. I don't know why, and I don't know who abducted her. All I know is that it seems to be the work of the Xmas Day Butcher."

Detective Castillo looked at me suspiciously—then her eyes scanned around my house; her expression softened slightly. "You should've told the police immediately, Lenny, but all right. We don't need to dwell on that," she said sternly. "We'll put out a missing persons report. I'll get a patrol to canvas the area, though..." she sighed, glancing toward the frosted window. "In this shitty weather, I doubt anyone's getting far. But she's in danger—no doubt about that. We'll have to do our best."

"Thank you, detective. I appreciate it," I whispered.

She nodded slowly. "For your sake, I hope we find her and that this isn't another case that ends up like poor Clara."

I lowered my hands and clasped them together. "Do you think..." my mind was in deep thought, my forehead creased with lines of worry. "... Angela's abduction is related to Clara's disappearance?" I asked.

Her cold gaze lingered on me. "Oh, Clara St. Nicklaus," she sighed. "She went missing around Christmas last year. She vanished without a trace, like Angela. I hope it's not the same, Lenny," she said gravely.

I hoped that Angela's disappearance was not connected to Clara's. I remembered the flyers with her innocent face, the candlelight vigil, and the way people in Whisper's Creek started to move a little more quickly at night during the months that followed. It had been such a tragic, harrowing event. After weeks of trying to find her, all hope had been lost.

Rumors swirled around town that she had been murdered. Some believed it was the boyfriend—Henry. Others believed it was someone more sinister—a serial killer that left behind a mark relating to dolls. But the latter didn't fit the MO.

As the memory of Clara's tragedy faded, so did the cautions people took to ensure they wouldn't be next. That would all change now that Angela was gone, taken by a truly deranged monster.

The difference between them is that there wasn't a Xmas Day Butcher playing a sinister game with Clara; there was only one involving Angela...and me.

Whisper's Creek was a place of nightmares, a breeding ground for evil incarnate to suck people into darkness, never to be seen again. There was no help in this cursed town, only a deathly silence to questions that'd never be answered.

If Whisper's Creek were a person, it would be cruel, blind, and deaf—no heart, no mercy, and no justice existed here.

Castillo shifted closer to me, snapping me out of my frenzied, inner trance. She asked me something while lowering her voice. "Lenny, I have to ask...did you have anything to do with her disappearance?"

"No." The word came out harsher than I meant it to. "God, no. I'd never!" I pleaded, perhaps a bit too loudly and desperately.

Her focused eyes held my panicked stare, searching for something in my worried face. Perhaps she was searching for innocence...or guilt.

I'd never hurt Angela. She's the best thing that's ever happened to me.

She took a deep breath and straightened her back. "Okay, I'll get this box back to the lab as soon as possible. Maybe forensics can pull a print off them, but..." she shrugged. "We don't have much to work with, and in this weather, nothing's being done that quickly. I'm sorry. Roads are horrible and still blocked in. We don't have a lab here."

I nodded in appreciation. "It's alright, I understand."

When she left, the dreadful silence in my house felt loud and heavy around me. I remembered the image of the blood-streaked ornament in the gift box. It seemed to glisten faintly, taunting me—torturing my soul.

I tried to think about what I should do, but the harder I searched my memories for an answer, for a response I could give to this Xmas Day Butcher, the more they evaporated into blackness. My mind didn't want to go to that dark place, the one from my childhood. I had trained it for so many years to block everything out—all the pain, all the blood...all the death.

I never felt like I had settled in my life, I always bounced from place to place with my brother, Lincoln. From the orphanage, Mercy's Light, to being adopted by Peter and Maria Frost, then moving in with Corita, a sweet Spanish lady afterwards.

All I saw were nightmarish flashes: evil cackles from an old woman, a child screaming, blood splattering the white walls, a pointed yellow star as sharp as a blade, a decorated Christmas tree toppled over...

I always told myself it hadn't happened and that it had been a very bad dream. That's how I coped with it, and that's how I tricked myself into believing I was never there that fateful Christmas night, so many years ago, and now I had a hard time discerning reality from fiction.

I needed some air, even if it was cold as ice outside. I was losing my damn mind in that quiet, empty house. Only the occasional howling winds were keeping me company, reminding me that the world was still spinning—even with Angela gone.

I went to my bedroom and put on some proper winter attire—a red and green sweater with Christmas lights, a beanie that was labeled: *Sexy Santa* and my gingerbread man-themed snow boots that fit snugly around my feet.

The cold hit me hard when I stepped outside; it always did. As I went down the porch steps, I noticed that snow was falling now, coating the street in a white, fluffy blanket. The sun was setting, so that meant that the night would soon shroud me in its darkness.

I stood in front of my house, a few feet away, staring at the old houses, far off in the distance, amongst the white nothingness that overtook us all in my little corner of town.

I was so still that I could hear the soft rhythm of my heartbeat—and then, somewhere at the edge of the yard to the left, there was movement. A dark figure—motionless, watching me.

I slowly turned my head to see it properly. "Hello?" my voice cracked in the winds that suddenly picked up. "Who's there?"

I took a step forward, and the figure shifted, slipping deeper into the white blur beyond the tree line, near the forest behind my house. I was terrified of who it was, but I needed to find Angela.

I'm not afraid of you, Xmas Day Butcher, if you're even real.

I walked after it, my snow boots crunching in the snow—it started to move deeper into the woods. I walked faster and decided to run, but my foot got caught on something buried in the snow, causing me to fall. I hit the ground hard, the snow breaking my fall. By the time I scrambled back up, the dark figure was gone.

It either escaped, or it was never there at all, and I was losing it.

I felt like I was suffocating as my breath became short and irregular. I was cracking under the pressure of Angela's disappearance. I needed to get my mind off it, just for a few hours, to feel sane again.

I then remembered that I had work to do. George's bathroom cabinets weren't going to fix themselves, and keeping my hands busy was better than chasing dark figures in the distance and thinking about horrific possibilities—possibilities that involved Angela with a person named "The Xmas Day Butcher."

George was probably irate with me, and undoubtedly, I had thirty missed calls from him. I'd have to explain to him the horrible situation I was in. I only hoped he'd sympathize with me, especially with his own daughter still missing.

Who knows if they'll ever find that poor girl...if she's still alive.

Whisper's Creek looked like something out of a Christmas post-card as I walked down Lochlear Lane, gloved hands in my pockets, nearing the town square. I saw snow falling on the rooftops of the town's shops, and garlands were draped over every door I passed. Kids from the local school laughed as they played in the snow in a fenced-in playground. It was situated in a far corner of the plaza, adjacent to the path I walked to get to the center of town.

I even heard the faint sound of a choir singing inside some faraway church; their voices were soothing—angelic. I tried to listen to it to calm myself down. I wanted to embrace the Christmas spirit, but I had a hard time doing so. Even more so, now that Angela was gone.

The choir only served to remind me of the white, abandoned church that sat on the opposite side of the forest near my home. Lincoln and I had seen it once, when we lived in Mercy's Light, the orphanage. It reminded him of that dreadful place. He always fantasized about burning it to the ground.

I couldn't blame him.

Everything felt hollow in Whisper's Creek, and the Christmas joy that used to subtly hum through me because of Angela had been sucked out of me, leaving me to hate the town even more. I promised myself that when I found her, I'd convince her to leave this dreadful town, once and for all.

The entire time I walked to George's, I hoped that Detective Castillo would be able to find something on Angela's deranged ab-ductor—a fingerprint, a strand of hair—any trace of DNA that could point us in the right direction.

Hopefully the roads would clear out so that she'd be able to take that to a forensics lab.

By the time I reached George's place on the outskirts of town, my fingers were numb, despite wearing gloves, and my thoughts were darker than the blackening sky above.

His farmhouse looked like it had risen from the snow, like a haunted house. It had a sagging porch, fading paint, and a barn that leaned to one side.

George was waiting on the porch, shaking in the cold, an angry scowl carved deep into his face.

"You're late, Lenny! Where the hell have you been?!" he barked.

I waved at him innocently as I walked up his porch steps. "I know, I'm sorry." I made it to the top and rubbed my hands together for warmth as he stared at me like I was a gremlin. "I have a good reason."

He scoffed, looking away in disgust. "So irresponsible," he grumbled. "What could it possibly be, Lenny?"

I took in a deep breath and looked at him straight in the eye. "Something's happened, George. Angela's missing."

The anger fell from his face like a ghostly Halloween mask. "Missing?" he asked, tone urgent. "My god, Lenny. Are you serious? How did that happen? Have you called the police?"

I sighed heavily. I still didn't know how it happened or why. "Detective Castillo was at my house. They're putting out a missing persons report."

George stared past me, out at the snowfall. "Clara," he said quietly. "It's just like Clara all over again. My goodness gracious."

I didn't know what to say, so I remained quiet. I didn't want it to be another case similar to Clara's. I couldn't live without Angela.

I didn't understand what I had done to deserve this cruel punishment, and with Christmas around the corner as well. I thought my childhood had been punishment enough—that I had already gone through all the suffering a single human being could endure. What I learned later is that it never really ends—suffering, that is.

We all had to find ways to cope and to continue to endure, because no one was above it.

No one.

It must've been planned for years. He must've been watching me all this time—how I loved and cherished Angela. The Xmas Day Butcher knew where to strike me where it hurt most: my beloved wife.

Was I the perfect victim? Was I a job that needed to be finished?

"Do you think..." he swallowed hard. "Do you think that whoever's behind this could be the same person who took Clara? Could my daughter still be alive?"

I crossed my arms and pondered the question. "I don't know," I admitted. "But something's definitely going on, and it's not good. Someone left messages for me. Bloody ornaments and a letter that warned me that I needed to play some game. My deadline is Christmas Day to find my wife."

George's eyes narrowed. "What game? Who sent you this? Lenny, this is insane. I can't believe this is happening to you."

I looked out at the snow-covered field in the distance. George was right—it really was insane. "This person calls themselves..." I hesitated, the words struggling to come out as I spoke them, "The Xmas Day Butcher."

Suddenly, the cold winds howled around the farmhouse, rattling the loose wooden boards and pushing the snowfall all around us. It was an omen.

For a heartbeat, George didn't move, then he let out a humorless chuckle. "A butcher? On Christmas Day?"

His haunted eyes searched mine, something fearful behind them. "You don't think...no, that's impossible. He's been dead for years. It happened a long time ago."

I immediately knew what he was referring to.

"Unless," I whispered, "what if it's a copycat killer?"

George tore his eyes away from me, tightly shut his lips, and refused to say another word.

CHAPTER 4
DECEMBER 4TH

I sat on my living room floor, legs crossed, the dying glow of the Christmas tree illuminating me in red and green, subtly mimicking my deteriorating state of mind. I was trying to forget my last conversation with George; it brought me nothing but pain.

The house felt so cold and abandoned without Angela—it was too quiet and too empty. She always brought the warmth.

Every ornament on the tree was like a ghostly memory of our time together throughout the years. If I weren't able to find her, they'd remain as shattered, visual fragments of our relationship, floating aimlessly in my already tormented head.

Oh, how I missed her. I missed the way she hummed Christmas songs when she cooked our delectable Christmas dinner, the way she teased me with her Christmas underwear by draping it over my face, and the way she always insisted on putting every single ornament she could find on the Christmas tree until it nearly weighed it down to the floor.

She was silly like that, and she brought that out of me. I needed that—after everything I had gone through.

My hand drifted underneath the tree, reaching out to grab a dusty snow globe that had a winter wonderland inside. I pulled it out and shook it—the wonderland was suddenly engulfed in white. Something about that snow globe unlocked a memory, one from many years ago—one of my first interactions with Angela.

I found myself back there: at my high school in Gravestone. It was the town closest to Whisper's Creek—that town was more of a civilized place, but expensive. It only got worse over the years.

Little hills of snow crunched under my boots as I crossed the courtyard, my breath leaking from my lips in little white clouds. It was my lunch period, and I'd chosen the far bench by the water fountain near a vending machine—an area no one else ever sat in. I loved the quiet there. I needed the calm; my mind was often too frantic—too chaotic. I always thought I'd snap, like I was destined to do so.

I sat down on the bench and pulled out a sandwich from my bag when the first snowball hit me square in the chest. A second volley was beamed at the back of my neck.

"Hey, freak boy!" one of them yelled; obnoxious laughter followed.

I tried to ignore it, but that never worked. High school kids were relentless and unforgiving—especially the bullies.

Another snowball smashed into the side of my head, nearly knocking my glasses off. I slid off my backpack and used it to protect my face. I wasn't good at standing up for myself, and besides, I had zero backup, no friends.

"Look at this loser," one of them sneered. "What's he even doing in school? Shouldn't he be institutionalized? The dude's a damn psycho."

They circled me, four of them, cheeks red from the cold, their ugly faces twisting with cruel smiles. My heart thudded hard against my ribs. I hated how tiny I felt next to them, how powerless and full of fear I was in their presence.

But then, someone decided to save me. I still didn't understand why, but she was just like that—a kind soul, an angel that had descended from the heavens above to change my life for the better.

Her stern voice cut through the air. "Scram." It was Angela, tall and angelic—with dark, shoulder-length hair and piercing brown eyes. She stood a few feet away from them, her arms crossed, her intense gaze fixated on them.

The boys shifted uncomfortably away from me, growing quiet all of sudden. I could see the fear in their blank faces. "What's up, Angela?" one asked like a mouse.

She came closer, making herself known as someone who was not to be trifled with. "You'll be up on the roof—when I throw you up there." She gave him a devious smile. "Would you like that?"

The bully muttered something in another language while shaking his head. "No, that's cool. We're all good here. Just don't tell the principal, please." He signaled for his friends to follow him away from me.

"Why are we leaving? She's just a girl," one whispered. "She's not just a girl; she'll kick my ass. What am I gonna do? Kick it back? Don't be a toilet shithead," the head bully hissed back.

She walked over and sat down next to me without missing a beat. I finally let my guard down, my face red from having a pretty girl stand up for me. I didn't feel like I deserved that. I should've been able to stand up for myself, but I always appreciated Angela for doing that.

Still, I should've been a man, or what was considered being a man. It was a personal thing—nothing to do with anyone else or how society viewed the relationship between men and women. I needed to have enough self-respect to defend my honor. Angela opened my mind to this change I needed to instill in myself.

I opened my mouth, almost afraid to speak—the words stuck in my throat. "Hey...thank you. Thank you for doing that; that was really nice of you."

She turned to me and playfully punched my arm. "I got you. I don't like seeing people bullying others." She flipped her gorgeous hair, and a few strands hit my face, but I didn't care. I even kind of liked it. "It's freaking lame, and those guys are always dogging you. I thought it was high time someone did something."

I nodded in appreciation; it was true. They bullied and teased me for nearly my entire high school life. I was an easy target for them until Angela came along.

"Why do they bother you so much anyway? What's up with them?" she asked.

"There's...stupid rumors; I'm sure you've heard about them," I muttered, brushing snow off my shoulder.

She gave me a curious look. "I'm sorry, what rumors?"

I hesitated. "About me and my family."

I knew that she knew what I was talking about, but she didn't want to pry. Nearly everyone in the school knew what had happened; there was no way she didn't know.

We had spoken a few times in class, just casual conversations, nothing about our personal lives. That's how she knew me and how shy I was. I was sure that she felt immense pity for me. I could tell by the way she looked at me when she passed me in the hall—with soft, downcast eyes and a kind smile.

Angela's eyes patiently searched mine. "Where are you from, anyway? I don't think I've ever asked that. Were you born here?" she was kind enough to change the subject.

I gulped and squirmed next to her; my body didn't know how to react to a pretty girl in close proximity. "No I wasn't. I was placed in an orphanage here and I was adopted. Before that...I bounced around a lot in Central America." She continued to look at me, interested in what I was saying, silently encouraging me to tell my story, even though she probably already knew it. I always loved that about her. "Long story short, my parents were taken by criminals when I was younger. I never saw them again."

Her face softened. "Oh no, Lenny." She affectionately grabbed my arm. "I'm so sorry."

I forced a dry laugh. "Yeah, I'm sure you don't want to hear any-more."

She squeezed my arm and nodded. "You can tell me if you want to. I'm listening to you."

I couldn't believe the treatment I was receiving from her. Sure, we'd spoken before, but never like this. I wondered what compelled her to do so. Maybe it dawned on her that I desperately needed a friend, someone who'd listen to me, and maybe she needed that, too.

I cleared my throat and continued. "Before my parents were taken, they managed to send us to the States to live with a relative, my father's distant cousin. Things didn't work out with her, so we got dumped in this place called Mercy's Light. It was run by this witch, Mildred. She wanted everything silent—no music, no games. Just quiet—always quiet. My brother Lincoln and I...we hated it, and her."

Angela tilted her head. "You had a brother?"

I never talked about him, but she knew that I did. I concluded that she wanted to act like she knew nothing about me because she didn't want to assume anything about my life; there had been a lot of nasty rumors, and many of them were simply not true.

"Yeah, his name was Lincoln. He didn't last long there. Neither of us did. We then got adopted by an older couple named Peter and Maria Frost. They weren't as bad as Mildred, but they didn't care much about us either. They did the bare minimum—kept us inside most of the time, like they were allergic to kids. It was horrible, but at least we had a place to live."

I remembered pausing my life's story there, my throat tightening before I added the last part to it—the tragedy. I didn't know if she wanted to hear about that.

"What happened next...it's really terrible. I don't have to tell you. It's just...sad. It's really sad," I said quietly.

She placed her hand gently on my lap. "You can tell me if you want to. I'm here for you." I glanced at her, and her face was serious. I could tell she was telling the truth, and I felt strangely comforted by her, like I could tell her anything in the whole world and she wouldn't judge me for it.

"Eventually...Colton Kilhouser happened. The man they called the Xmas Day Butcher."

Her brow furrowed. "I've heard of him, but I haven't read much into it. I don't like bad news."

I took a deep breath. "Well, he's the man who killed them—my brother and my foster parents. He broke into our house and...slashed them with a Christmas star. Why? I have no idea. Somehow, I survived the massacre. He was on the run for a few days, but eventually they caught him and put him in an institution: the Gibraltar Institute. He was declared insane, or something like that. He died there in an accident, not long after he went in. But by then..." I trailed off, the words weighing heavily in my chest.

Angela touched my shoulder gently. "That's horrible, I'm so sorry. I don't even know what to say."

"It's fine. I'm just trying to drift along, trying to keep my spirits up."

As I turned to look at her, really look at her, her eyes were misty as she frowned at me, a deep expression of melancholy on her face. She slowly wrapped her arms around me and hugged me tight. I did the same.

I hadn't felt affection in such a long time; I even forgot what it was supposed to feel like, but with Angela, my heart swelled with warmth. I felt seen—I felt heard. Maybe that's why she wanted to hear me tell my tragic story; she wanted to connect with me.

As we let go, I was eager to change the depressing subject. I didn't want my sadness to linger in the corners of my mind; the death of my family had burdened my heart enough.

I forced a happy grin. "But hey, I live with an old lady now, Corita. It's some kind of normal, I guess. Except when she throws a flying "chancla" at me for leaving dishes in the sink. That can be pretty frightening."

Angela laughed; she sounded so bright and joyful. She had dark features, but she glowed like the sun, and it had already begun to rub off on me. My feelings for her were growing stronger by the minute. I always had a crush on her—I was an admirer from afar, never daring to make a move.

How could I? My life had been dark and heavy—full of death and torment. I never wanted to bring anyone else into that, so I told myself that I was destined to be alone.

Until a sliver of light, shining through the cracks of the dark wall I had constructed in my mind, powered through, enveloping me in its love. I considered it nothing short of a miracle, a gift bestowed upon me for enduring everything I had gone through. All the horrible things I had to witness and stomach, just to stay alive in this cruel world.

She giggled; it made my heart sing. "That lady sounds like my *abuela*. My grandma."

"She can be mean, but she makes the best empanadas," I said, tempted to lick my fingers. "They're the best I've ever had, and I had plenty in a few countries in Central America: like Guatemala, Nicaragua, Honduras, El Salvador...but no one else in this cursed town can make food from Latin America to save their life. It's almost as depressing as all this snow."

She playfully shoved me, her face showing offense. "Hey! The snow is beautiful if you give it meaning. To me, it signifies Christmas. The most joyous holiday there is."

I scoffed. I didn't agree with her, but I was curious as to why she liked it. Most people were vain and only cared for the presents.

I opened my mouth, carefully formulating the words in my head before spitting them out, "Why do you like Christmas? Presents?" I stared at her as she studied the ground, squinting her eyes, thinking.

"You know," she began, "I love the idea of it. That there is this merry, joyous holiday at a time in the world with so much snow, ice, and cold. I think it's an interesting irony. It tells me that even in the darkest, coldest places of the world—the Christmas spirit can still be alive and warm...and wonderful." She beamed at me, her dimples showing. How could I not fall in love with her? She made it easy, too.

I stammered, not expecting that answer at all. "Wow, that's...amazing. You're a very cool person, Angela. That's a great reason for loving Christmas."

Angela's grin widened as she winked at me. "I'm Venezuelan, by the way. I know how to make them."

I stared at her, confused, my mind going blank because she had winked at me.

"W-what? Make what?"

She giggled at me again; her laugh was so adorable, and I was sure it had the power to cure my depression forever.

"Empanadas, you *Silly Billy*. What did you think I was talking about?"

She even knew how to make empanadas. I swear, my heart nearly stopped.

Oh my god, marry me, my Spanish queen, I thought.

She tilted her head playfully. "Maybe I'll even bring you some—only if you hang out with me for Christmas. So you better say yes." She winked at me again.

Am I dreaming?

I blubbered before answering. "Yes, okay. Please," I said too quickly. I caught myself and tried to play it cool. "I mean...yeah, that's like super chill. I'd like that."

Her smile lingered, but then her eyes turned curious again. "So, I do have one question, and you don't have to answer, but...the rumors...the horrible tragedy that happened with your family...why do they bully you about it? How can they be so cruel? I don't understand."

I stared at the snow that had begun to fall all around us. I was taken back to that day for a brief moment, in my old house. The Christmas tree, the white walls, the wrapped presents...all stained with blood. Peter, Maria, and Lincoln Frost...lying dead on the ground—throats slashed. The masked monster from my nightmares coldly stared at me, dead in the eyes, before escaping.

He had spared me, and I wasn't sure why. The question had swirled in my head since that very day, when my entire life flashed before my eyes. On that day, my life had truly ended. I was convinced of that.

"Because..." I swallowed down a nervous lump in my throat. "They think that Colton Kilhouser is a lie—a made-up boogeyman for the papers. They never released any photos of him, only odd sketches. It was a name they could blame for the massacre to protect me. Why? Well...people always questioned how I survived. So, they think that I'm the person who killed my family."

CHAPTER 5
DECEMBER 5TH

The snow kept coming down like it wanted to bury the whole damn town, and maybe it should've, once and for all. I was riding with Detective Castillo into town in an effort to find Angela and to spread the word.

The police car's wipers squeaked uselessly against the windshield, smearing more snow than they cleared. Eventually, she turned them off.

The roads that led out of Whisper's Creek were sealed in a shell of ice, and every other officer in Whisper's Creek was either busy keeping cars from skidding into ditches or helping the ones that had already fallen into one. That meant we were on our own.

"I appreciate this," I told her, voice low. "I know you're stretched thin."

Castillo just nodded, eyes locked on the road. She looked tired, same as me, but there was steel in her—she was tough. "We'll find her, Lenny. We have to. We can't just leave it to the wind and let this freak win."

When we pulled into the square and parked, I almost forgot why we were there. The town was wrapped in lights and color, like there was a Christmas festival taking place. Giant plastic candy canes embedded into the snow, lifelike Santas propped up near the retail stores, and a fully decorated Christmas tree in the center of the plaza with every ornament you could think of—glass balls and sparkling angels that shimmered in the light, metallic ribbons and artificial snowflakes that complemented the rest of the tree.

As we stepped out of the car, the sweet aroma of chocolate chip cookies and cinnamon drifted out from the bakery across the street from us.

Angela loved all of it, and she would've wanted to see all of this. I needed to find her before it was too late. Even if I had to play their sinister game. I refused to spend Christmas without her.

Castillo and I went from shop to shop, showing people the photo of Angela on her phone, asking if anyone had seen a woman in a red coat with dark hair, about five-foot-six. The answers were all the same—shakes of the head, worried looks, polite no's. I followed her, half-focused on the people we were asking for information and half-lost in thought, while I maneuvered around hills of piled-up snow.

The last time I saw Angela was on the morning of December 1st. I tried to think of why she could've been abducted, but no answers were coming to mind. It just didn't make sense. It must've had something to do with me.

I tried to tell myself she was just fine—that I'd find her before Christmas Day and everything would go back to normal. But the truth was, Whisper's Creek was a strange town, and it felt like the type of place where people went missing and never returned. I thought about Clara, and that's what frightened me the most.

"Lenny? 'Sup homie."

The familiar voice caused a chill up my spine. I turned around reluctantly.

Joseph was standing near the giant Christmas tree in the center of the square, a duffel bag with jingle bell symbols draped all over it strapped across his shoulder. His dark blue work coat was zipped all the way up, and his eyes examined me with concern.

"Dude, I heard," he said, walking toward me slowly. "Angela's missing? What the hell is that all about? That's wild as hell!"

I nodded, my jaw tightly clenched. "Yeah, it's been the worst. She wasn't home later that day, on December 1st—when I went shopping for her Christmas gift."

His face scrunched up with worry, and he looked like someone had punched him in the gut. "Holy shit, Lenny. That's so awful. I can't believe it. Where could she have gone?"

I couldn't believe it either, and I couldn't tell him about the Xmas Day Butcher, not yet anyway. I already made the mistake of telling George, and Detective Castillo scolded me for it. She wanted to keep it tight-lipped—she didn't need the town panicking into chaos.

Especially when there already had been a Xmas Day Butcher, so many years ago.

Besides, I didn't entirely trust Joseph.

"We've been asking the whole town," I sighed. "I'm hoping she's just holed up somewhere; maybe she got lost because the roads are blocked coming into town. Anything but..." I trailed off, unwilling to say what I feared most.

Joseph nodded slowly, his eyes looking me up and down. There was a pause before he asked, in a soft tone, "You two...were things okay between you? Everything good at home?"

The question hung between us like a thick fog. I couldn't believe he had just asked that. "*Of course, everything is fine, you damn idiot!*" That's what I wanted to yell into his smug face, but I chose to keep my temper in check.

My stomach tightened. "I'm sorry, I don't know what you mean. We were just fine. We weren't fighting or anything. Is that what you were wondering?"

He'd better back off before he says something else that's just as idiotic.

"No, I didn't mean—" he started, holding up a hand, indicating peace. "I know that married couples fight. Shit happens, man. It's happened to me, too. But did she ever talk about leaving you or anything?"

I took a step toward him, not believing that he was continuing with his intrusive line of questioning. "No, she did not. She never would." I angrily pointed a finger at his face. "I had nothing to do with her going missing—if that's what you're getting at."

Joseph flinched backwards, taken aback by my harsh reaction.

Yeah, that's right. I'm not rolling over, buddy. Especially when you talk to me in an accusatory manner.

He awkwardly stared down at the snow, his free hand sliding into his pocket. "I'm sorry, dude. I didn't mean to accuse you of anything.

It's just...she's a good woman. She's so kind and beautiful. I just can't picture her disappearing without saying something first. That's just not who she is as a person. I do work with her."

I folded my arms, staring into his eyes with intent. "I know exactly who she is, trust me. I'm married to her."

He chuckled, trying to diffuse the rising tension between us. "You're right, bud. You would know."

"I'd never hurt her, and I never have," I said flatly. "That's the honest truth. I swear on my dead brother's name."

He looked up at me then, his face now pale, his lips pressed together, not knowing what to say next.

"Alright, man," he said. "I believe you. I do. I'll keep my eyes open for you. I'll ask around at work; maybe someone saw her."

"I appreciate it, Joseph," I muttered. I barely meant it.

He turned to leave but paused after a few steps. "Hey, Lenny?" he asked over his shoulder. "If you hear anything...please let me know. Will you?"

I stared at his back. "Yeah, sure thing."

He walked off, shoulders slumped. I watched him until he disappeared behind the row of stores that faced the lot.

I wanted to believe that he was worried, that he truly cared about Angela's well-being and how she had gone missing, but something was off.

I didn't appreciate the way he was insinuating things about our marriage. The way his wide, pervasive eyes stared at me like I had something to do with Angela's disappearance.

Whatever was going on, I had the feeling that Joseph knew more than he was letting on, but without any proof, I couldn't do jack shit about it.

I searched around for Detective Castillo and found her talking to a group of residents building a snowman.

I decided to go into a Christmas store on the corner, a few feet away from me. The bell over the door jingled, and the warm air brought me great relief. The place was packed with Christmas mugs, ugly sweaters, and an assortment of candies like candy canes and gumdrops. Behind the counter stood a woman in her sixties, her hands wrapped around a hot mug of cocoa.

"Good evening," I said, trying to sound casual. "Have you seen this woman around anywhere? She's my wife." I showed her Angela's picture on my phone.

She squinted and frowned. "Can't say that I have, hon. Why? You think she's gone missing?"

"Yes, I'm hoping she's alright."

The woman hesitated, then leaned in slightly, her voice dropping. "You don't think it's connected, do you?"

I arched an eyebrow in curiosity. "Connected to what?"

"To that other girl who disappeared—Clara St. Nicklaus. She went missing last year around Christmas. Some say it was the boyfriend, Henry, or maybe a killer. Henry's dead, but what about Clara? Could she be with Angela somewhere?"

It felt like a block of ice slid down my spine. Whatever fate had been thrust upon Clara, I hoped it wouldn't be the same for Angela. "Right…Clara. She was never found. I don't know. The whole thing's so murky and terrible."

George's beloved daughter.

The woman's eyes darted to the windows, where snow was falling against the glass. "You've heard the rumors, haven't you?"

"No. What rumors?"

She lowered her voice even more, like there was a ghost that might eavesdrop on us. "They say her father, George, snapped one night and killed her. Just like that man who butchered that family on Christmas Day twenty years ago. Colton Kilhouser—the man they called *The Xmas Day Butcher*."

She didn't know that the family she was talking about was my family. It had been so long ago, and I never brought it up—ever. I tried to erase my past as best I could. I lived in seclusion and rarely ever spoke with anyone in town. Only George knew that that had been my family. Thankfully, he kept quiet about it.

That damn name twisted something deep inside me, like a serrated knife. I hadn't heard it in years, and yet it still haunted me, long after the dark deed had been done.

The woman continued, "George knew that couple, you know. Peter and Maria Frost. Two boys were there as well—I forget their names, but one died and one survived. I don't know where the survivor went off to—maybe an institution." I was shocked that I didn't end up in one, to be fair. "George used to bring them hams every Christmas. They say the murders were a result of a curse—*The Curse of Whisper's Creek*."

I didn't answer right away; that name was now stuck in my mind, and my thoughts were in disarray because of it. I felt like I was about to black out while I tried to work past the heart-shredding pain I had gone through so many years earlier.

Colton Kilhouser. The first Xmas Day Butcher.

That name wasn't just a piece of lore tied to this cursed town. It was the black hole in my memory—the one I'd spent twenty years pretending didn't exist. That sick, twisted monster killed my foster parents and my brother, Lincoln. They kept telling me that I was too young to remember, but I did. I remembered the screams, the blood, the ominous silence in the aftermath, and the way those monster's eyes stared up at me—with no life behind them.

When I moved in with Corita—the sweet old woman who spoke to me in Spanish—I tried to start over, but the kids at school wouldn't let me. They said I killed my family myself. They said I was a psychopath.

The press and the media never showed any photos of Colton Kilhouser—only sketches and drawings. It was all very hush-hush, like it was a cover-up. But I was a barely functioning kid at that point. What did I know?

The bullies told me that Leonard Frost wasn't even my real name—that my actual name was Colton Kilhouser. One of the most ridiculous conspiracy theories I've ever heard in my life. If I murdered my family, I'd remember.

I took off my gloves and rubbed my hands together for warmth, trying to shake off the ice-cold chill that that name gave me. Colton

Kilhouser was supposed to be long dead. That's the part I didn't understand about this "Xmas Day Butcher." The part I refused to acknowledge.

I had tried so hard, for so long, to forget that name—to erase it from my mind forever. When it came back, I refused to believe that he still existed. I didn't understand how Colton Kilhouser had come back from the dead. It was impossible. The only possible explanation: a copycat killer. But why? Why now? Why is there a return of the Xmas Day Butcher?

A scream ripped through the plaza, echoing throughout the air, shattering the calm. Our heads jerked towards the window, eyes wide, immediately alarmed at whatever the hell was going on.

I spotted Detective Castillo running across the plaza towards the noise outside. I threw myself out the door and followed, my boots almost slipping on the ice. A small crowd of concerned townsfolk had gathered near a streetlight. An elderly woman stood frozen—pointing at something, her face paler than the snow falling around us.

"I—I'm sorry," she stammered. "You told me about that missing woman, and I got scared."

Castillo tried to calm her. "It's alright, ma'am, just take a breath."

My eyes followed her pointed finger. A Christmas stocking hung from the streetlight on a string—it gently swayed in the wind.

Something about it didn't feel right at all. I stepped closer, grabbed it, and tugged softly. It was heavy.

I glanced at Castillo. "Should I..." my heart nervously thumped against my chest, "...check what's inside?"

She nodded.

I pulled on it and broke the string that it was connected to. I slowly peeked inside, and as soon as I did, I dropped it in horror.

"What is it?!" Castillo asked frantically.

I turned to her. "It's a goddamn foot," I whispered, my voice trembling.

It was a severed foot. It was as white as ice, frozen and stuffed inside the stocking. The woman screamed again, and so did everyone else in the crowd as they dispersed and ran off.

CHAPTER 6
DECEMBER 6TH

I didn't sleep that night. Every time I closed my eyes, I saw the Christmas stocking swinging in the wind, the severed foot stuffed inside. The foot had Christmas-colored nails—red and green. Detective Castillo had confirmed that with me.

Angela had painted hers just like that before she vanished. She'd been smiling when she did it, sitting on the couch, humming some Christmas carol under her breath.

Now that image made me want to puke my guts out. That son of a bitch had chopped off her foot, stuffed it inside a stocking, and swung it over a streetlamp for the entire town to see, like some demented Christmas prop.

It was already morning, and I barely slept a wink. The snow had calmed, but the world outside my window was still as white and dead as the day Angela went missing. Detective Castillo safely stored the severed foot for the forensics lab, but who knew if it'd make it there in time.

The silence in my house felt heavy, and ever since yesterday, it felt like the whole town was now holding its breath. Everyone knew something was wrong now, but Castillo still wanted to keep a lid on things for as long as possible. She didn't want people to know that a deranged lunatic was on the loose in Whisper's Creek.

I stepped outside to get out of my head for a bit, if that would even be possible, and that's when I noticed the gift box.

Jesus Christ, another one.

It was calmly sitting on my porch—a neat little thing wrapped in shimmery green paper, and tied with a red ribbon. The freak must've been dropping them off at my house in the middle of the night. How the hell did they withstand the cold?

I felt a twitch in my neck, and the air seemed to thicken as I crouched down to pick it up. It was quite heavy as I brought it inside to set it on my coffee table.

This better not be her damn head or something.

I opened the drawer of the table and pulled out a box cutter. I flipped the blade out and carefully tore the wrapping paper along the top, where the ribbon was. I ripped it off and lifted the lid to the box.

The smell was immediately apparent; a noxious scent of sour ham and metal attacked my nostrils.

I saw the white note first, embedded in some giant round ball of...flesh?!

I grabbed the note and then read the words that were scrawled in jagged black ink: **CLUE #3**: *"Learn who I am, or Angela becomes a Christmas ham."*

My stomach dropped to the floor.

In the gift box was a ham—gray and slimy with mold, stinking of rot. As I examined it closer, there was something stuck inside it, like some kind of twisted garnish. It was a metallic Christmas star.

I stumbled back, choking on the horrific smell. My body began trembling, and I could barely hold my composure.

That star—five-pointed, sharp, golden—it wasn't random. It meant something. This monster definitely knew who I was—he knew this was the weapon that was used to butcher my family. I was being tormented, played with...but why? Why me?! What had I done?! Why punish Angela?!

The image of the severed foot flashed again in my mind as I fell to the floor. I remembered the painted nails: red and green. I could almost see a masked monster chopping off Angela's foot as she screamed—a sharp axe plunging downward into her ankle, the bones crunching, the blood spilling out of the fresh wound like a crimson fountain. A twisted man dressed as Santa Claus, having his way with her, to destroy me.

I tightly shut my eyes, tears flowing out of them, my gut broiling with fire. I curled into a ball, feeling hopeless and helpless. I had no idea how to help my poor, dear Angela. The idea of her being butchered—of what might be left of her when I found her—was enough to make me dizzy.

I angrily slammed my fist against the cold floor, pain erupting along my arm. Whoever was doing this wanted me ruined forever. They wanted me to remember them. It was happening all over again—all the suffering and the anguish that I had felt when the first Xmas Day Butcher slaughtered my family, all those years ago.

I couldn't take it—I couldn't handle it. I closed my eyes even tighter, secretly hoping it was a cruel nightmare that'd be over as soon as I woke up.

I jolted awake to the sound of banging on my door. I was in my lounge chair, my legs sprawled out, the taste of air on my tongue—I had fallen asleep. I quickly checked my watch—it was still December 6th.

I rubbed my dry eyes and slid over to the front door to see who was there. When I checked the peephole, Detective Castillo was standing there, with a concerned look on her face.

Christ, did I call her again without knowing?

I took out my phone from my pocket and checked the call log—sure enough, I did call her. The call lasted around three minutes.

I must've called her about the "gift" I received before blacking out. I tended to have those episodes once in a blue moon, but now they were becoming more frequent...and my grip on reality was shifting away from me.

I swung open the door and stepped aside so she could enter. "Jesus, Lenny. You look like hell. Are you okay?"

I sighed heavily, hanging my head. "My wife's missing, and there's a man named the Xmas Day Butcher cutting up body parts and parading them in front of the town. What do you think?" I asked aloud. "I got another gift, by the way. But I'm sure I told you that over the phone."

When she saw the ham, her stony expression changed to complete horror. She reached inside her pocket and put on gloves to examine it. She lifted the note first, eyes narrowing as she read it. Then she looked back at the ham.

"Christmas ham, yellow Christmas star," she murmured. "That's not random."

I knew what she was getting at, but I wanted to see what she said. "What do you mean?"

She hesitated, glancing at me with worrisome eyes. "I didn't want to accept it, but it might be what I've been fearing since this whole thing started. Colton Kilhouser. A killer from Whisper's Creek, it was about twenty years ago now. The newspapers dubbed him: *The Xmas Day Butcher*. He killed the Frost family. This can be a copycat killer, because Colton's dead."

I paced back and forth. "I also didn't want to accept it, but here we are—dealing with someone who's seemingly come back from the dead, huh?"

Castillo shook her head, confused about what was going on. "He's been dead for years; this doesn't make any sense." She looked at me—square in the eyes. "Why would someone be sending this to you?"

I didn't want to say the possibility out loud because somehow that would've made it true, in my mind. But I knew that I needed to say it because it was clear that Detective Castillo did not know who I was, and maybe that'd help her catch this deranged sicko.

"Maybe because I was there," I said quietly. "I'm the kid whose foster parents he killed. He also killed my brother, Lincoln. I'm the lone survivor."

Her mouth parted slightly. "Oh my god. How the hell didn't I see it? You're Leonard Frost. I guess...I guess I never thought that that kid would've ever stayed in Whisper's Creek. Frost is a common last name here, and...I thought you were halfway across the country, hiding somewhere."

I nodded. "It's been a very long time. I was 12 when Colton killed my family, and I'm 32 now. My hair changed after I buzzed it. It used to be wavy and a lighter shade of brown. I have facial hair now, and after a while...no one recognized me anymore." I sighed, taking a seat on the armrest of my lounge chair. "A lot of people moved out of this place when that happened. I wanted to do the same, but...I just never did. I lived with an old lady named Corita. I met Angela in high school, and she didn't want to leave, so we didn't."

I got up and stared at the ceiling, quietly wondering how I ended up in this hellish predicament. "I just tried to forget it ever happened, and I pretended it didn't. It worked for a while, but now...it's come back to haunt me."

Castillo just stared at me—stunned. "I read about that case, but it was sealed tight. Not many details. Just...whispers from other cops on what went down."

"Always secrets in this town, huh?" I asked. "Always secrets."

She shook her head, pursing her lips together. "I'm tired of the secrets." Castillo dug her hands into the ham, trying not to breathe it in too deeply.

I looked at her curiously. "Shouldn't you take this back somewhere official? To be examined?"

She glanced at me, clucking her tongue. "We don't have anywhere official for shit like this. We send it to Gravestone, and the roads are still blocked off. Lenny, we're on our own. If we want to get shit done, it's up to us."

Inside was another clue—Castillo pulled it out; it was a folded newspaper clipping, yellowed with age. She placed it beside the ham and smoothed it out, grimacing at the stains of ham she was smearing on it. I read it without touching anything.

The date was December 25th.

The headline read: **"A XMAS DAY BUTCHER STRIKES IN WHISPER'S CREEK—COUPLE AND CHILD FOUND DEAD."**

Peter and Maria Frost: my foster parents. The story detailed how Colton Kilhouser had evaded police for three days before his capture. It mentioned his transfer: "Colton Kilhouser, dubbed the 'Xmas Day Butcher,' will be admitted to the Gibraltar Institute under the supervision of Doctor Thomas T. Tuttle. He has been declared legally insane. Councilman Carl Hamonte endorsed the decision and signed off on the transfer."

Hmm...Councilman Carl Hamonte is now Mayor Hamonte. That's Angela's boss.

I found it strange that there was nothing about me. No mention of a surviving son. "They erased me," I whispered. "I should be grateful; I guess it was for my own protection."

Castillo frowned. "This institute—Gibraltar. I've heard that name."

"I have too," I said. "It's some kind of mental hospital, right?"

"It is," she said. "But it's closed right now to visitors. We couldn't get there now anyway—not in this weather. Too much ice on the roads."

I nodded slowly, scanning the newspaper clipping again. My eyes found a grainy black-and-white photo at the bottom—a smiling family beside a Christmas tree. My foster parents, Peter and Maria Frost, and standing next to them, arm around Peter's shoulder, was George St. Nicklaus.

I suddenly remembered how George loved Christmas hams. How bizarre that the Xmas Day Butcher had sent me a moldy ham of all things.

I wonder...is George hiding anything?

CHAPTER 7
DECEMBER 7TH

I was curled up in bed that morning, fluffy sheets wrapped around me, the mug of hot cocoa warm between my hands, trying to scrub that disgusting ham out of my head. Detective Castillo had taken it back to the police station to put in evidence, and I was forever grateful for that.

I'd even tossed in a few marshmallows inside my cocoa, watching them melt into little white ghosts, remembering how Angela loved to drink the stuff.

"How the hell can I be sipping hot cocoa at a time like this?" I muttered to myself, a dry laugh escaping before I could stop it. Angela would giggle at me.

She always said I was the kind of guy who liked to sit in bed all day, covers draped over me, avoiding sunlight as much as I could. I took comfort in the darkness, in the stillness, in the quiet...

But now everything was different. I needed to play a sick man's game to get my wife back. The worst part was that there wasn't much I could do at the moment. I had to wait for him to drop off the "gifts" so that we'd complete whatever cycle he had begun in the first place. I just hoped Angela was okay, and that if the Xmas Day Butcher really did cut off her foot, I hoped he tended to her wound.

God, it was so horrible to think of my Angela without a foot. She did nothing to deserve that. This was a true monster in the making.

My thoughts refused to stay still; they drifted to my employer: George St. Nicklaus. I thought about him and Clara and how horrible it had been when she went missing—never to be found again. I was beginning to think there might've been a connection between her disappearance and Angela's. What if the Xmas Day Butcher had abducted them both?

Something about George didn't sit right with me. Supposedly, some townsfolk believed that he had "snapped" and killed Clara by accident. He then hid the body, and that was that.

But what if he'd seen something he wasn't supposed to? Maybe he'd been forced to keep quiet. Maybe he had been forced to pretend that he didn't know what had happened with Clara, or maybe...just maybe...George really did kill his only daughter in a rage. He was always controlling her—this was a fact.

As I stared at the marshmallows dissolving in my cocoa, I convinced myself that going to George's place might've provided me with some answers. It beat staying at home, doing nothing, and feeling sorry for myself. Angela wouldn't be found in our bedroom.

I set aside the cocoa, got up from my bed, and dressed myself in some much-needed winter attire. I grabbed some random ornaments, including some miniature Diet Dr. Spencer cans, from a half-opened box near the Christmas tree and stuffed them inside a cloth bag. I needed an excuse to visit Grumpy Claus.

As I walked outside towards the town square, I noticed that the snow had crusted into thick ridges along the road. That's what all the road blockage must've been about. I crossed into the plaza and quietly stared at the streetlamp that had the severed foot inside the hanging Christmas stocking.

The town's shopping plaza had turned into a ghost town after that incident—no one dared to go outside. No children were jumping and running in the playground, no adults were shopping in the stores, and the blinds to most shops were shut. Everyone had been spooked, and word spread like wildfire, even amongst the snow.

My frenzied, anxious thoughts seemed to accelerate the time I spent walking to the St. Nicklaus residence. As it came into view, I noticed smoke rising from his chimney, swirling clouds of gray puffing out into the white sky. He was home; he always was.

I never imagined myself living in a white, snow-covered land in the middle of nowhere like George, but as the years went by, I was starting to understand it. The serenity you had in seclusion was nice, but even I had to admit that living alone, with no real neighbors, was beginning to make me go nutty.

Another reason to leave Whisper's Creek as soon as possible was that I wanted to feel normal—be normal, in a place surrounded by normal folks with families, kids, regular jobs...no cursed towns, deranged serial killers, or severed limbs in sight.

I hopped up the creaky porch steps and knocked on his rickety front door. When George opened up, his face looked more weathered than ever—his eyes were bloodshot, and his forehead was creased with lines that hadn't been there the last time I'd seen him. It was like something had been keeping him up at night, perhaps thoughts of the Xmas Day Butcher coming to find him next, or something far more sinister.

"Oh, hey, Lenny," he said, surprised to see me. "I didn't expect a visitor. What are you doing here?"

"I figured you could use a hand putting up the Christmas tree," I said, lifting the small bundle of ornaments I'd brought. "I thought it couldn't hurt to have some company."

He squinted at me while giving me his signature grumpy look. "Boy, you know I like to be alone—especially during the holidays. I haven't put up the Christmas tree because there's no point...Clara's gone."

I gulped, trying to find a minimal spark in his eyes, a shred of kindness I could lean into in order to get inside his home. "I understand how you feel. It's just..." I started to choke up. "...ever since Angela's been gone, I've felt so hopeless, George. I'm alone...so alone. I just wanted to share some company with someone I know, even if you're my boss," I said quietly.

He studied me carefully, almost rolling his eyes. I expected that from him. "You should've called first." He hesitated, then stepped aside. "Clara would've liked to put up the damn tree," he muttered.

I nodded gratefully and entered his home. It was in serious neglect. A dusty bookshelf sat in the corner; several newspapers about Clara's mysterious disappearance were pinned to a brown board beside it. The black leather couches were peeling, and the color was fading. A few empty eggnog cartons were strewn about on the floor along with some beer bottles.

A giant Christmas rug with a Santa Claus figure stretched from the front door to the entrance of the kitchen, stained and dirty with black footprints.

The room was dark and dim, with only a single lightbulb hanging from the ceiling, providing a minimal, yellowish hue as lighting. Ever since Clara vanished, George just didn't care anymore—about life or anything else, so it seemed.

George begrudgingly pulled the medium-sized Christmas tree out of a small storage closet he had near the living room. "Don't remember this shit being this damn heavy, dammit!" he threw it on the floor, broken pine needles floating in the air.

I rushed over to help him before he got angrier. I wasn't sure if that was possible for someone I named "Grumpy Claus," but I thought about those rumors of him "snapping." Could he have murdered Clara? Was that even possible? Could there be a connection between Clara and Angela? That was yet to be seen, but I intended to find out.

Because it was clear that the Xmas Day Butcher knew me, somehow, and they may have been closer to me than I thought. That was the most terrifying notion I've had in my mind ever since Angela's disappearance.

We set up the tree in the corner of the living room, near the wooden stand with the TV and the shuttered window where George refused to have natural light shining through. He was a man of darkness and no light—through and through. Just like a bratty teenager who always wanted their door closed.

The tree leaned a little to the right, but neither of us bothered fixing it. I knew George wouldn't care, and I didn't bother to ask him about it. We hung various ornaments on it—red glass bulbs, tiny snowmen, some candy canes, and some miniature Diet Dr. Spencer cans. Those were my absolute favorites.

George didn't say much as we decorated the tree. He just kept looking at it with hollow eyes that were filled with sorrow, like he couldn't stop thinking about Clara.

But was it out of sadness...? Or guilt?

When I went to grab another handful of decorations from underneath his wooden center table, I felt something else—cold and metallic. When I looked under, it was a small metal lockbox, unlocked. I thought that was odd.

I looked at him and pointed to it. "Hey, George, what's this?"

He jerked his head towards me, his eyes narrowing. "Oh, that's nothing. Just some random shit. You can take a look—see if there's anything worth putting on this tree."

I pulled it out and flipped the latch open. I crouched down and examined the contents inside. I found several pieces of jewelry—trinkets, bracelets, rings, and necklaces that shimmered faintly in the dim lighting. But something made my stomach drop, something that made me question why George had it in his possession. There was a pair of reindeer earrings inside, the same type of pair that Angela had worn.

That was the first thing that the Xmas Day Butcher had ever sent me in that devious little gift box—bloodied. Maybe I was going insane, but then again—maybe I wasn't. I didn't know the identity of the Xmas Day Butcher, but I knew it must've been someone close to me.

Suspicion slipped through the tone of my voice. "George, where did you get these?" I raised them high and in between my fingers so he could see.

He looked at me and stiffened while hanging a glass ball at the top of the tree. "At a shop in town, I'm holding them for her." He cleared his throat. "For when Clara finally comes home."

My heart hammered in my ears. George knew something—he had to. I had to ask anyhow; he had lived in this town for a very long time, and I had no answers for Angela. I didn't know where she was, and I didn't know what the hell was going on.

I tossed the reindeer earrings back in the lockbox and stood up. "Do you know anything about the original Xmas Day Butcher? Do you know why he killed my foster parents and my brother? I know that his name was Colton Kilhouser and that he's been dead for years, but...I just don't know anything more than that. There has to be more, right?"

He hung a candy cane hesitantly in the middle of the tree; while staring into it, his mind raced with thoughts, his mouth slightly twitching as he thought about what to say. He sighed heavily and waddled near me to sit down in his favorite armchair.

He tiredly rubbed his eyes. "You shouldn't look into it too deeply, son. It was a tragedy what happened to Peter, Maria, and Lincoln. Such a tragedy," he said softly while staring off into nothing. "There's secrets in this damn town—secrets that can't come out. I made the mistake of asking around once. I wanted to know why your family was murdered. I wanted to know Colton Kilhouser's motive. I wanted some goddamn answers for my former neighbors." He shook his head. "There's powerful people in Whisper's Creek. They covered it all up. They covered up Colton Kilhouser's origin, the Frost family murders, Clara's disappearance... and they might be covering up Angela's as well."

That shook me to my core. I didn't know that George had asked around all those years ago. I never knew he'd be the type of guy to hold these kinds of answers. I figured he must've grown a bit soft after Clara vanished.

I ran a hand through my hair, so many thoughts racing and rushing through my head. It sounded like George thought that some sort of conspiracy was taking place in Whisper's Creek. "Who are these powerful people?" I asked carefully.

He rubbed his temples. "I think it has something to do with that whacko institute." He snapped his fingers at me. "That Gibraltar place. The doctor there...what was his name?"

"I believe it's Doctor Thomas T. Tuttle," I answered.

His eyes suddenly met mine. "Yes, him. He holds more power than you might think. He's buddy-buddy with Mayor Carl Hamonte.

Rumor is, Doctor Tuttle secretly funded all of his political campaigns."

Holy shit.

I crossed my arms. "Is that so?"

He leaned forward in his chair, his voice low, trembling. "Look, Lenny...I barely remembered that Peter and Maria had adopted two boys. I used to drop off Christmas hams for them every year, and we'd have some nice conversations. Sometimes, I'd come in and have some hot cocoa—maybe a cup of coffee—and I'd catch a glimpse of you sitting on top of the stairway, holding that little doll. Before I could say anything about you, you'd disappear. They never mentioned you guys; I don't know why. Maybe to protect you?"

The words sucker-punched me, knocking the wind out of my gut. I remembered that doll. It had been the only thing that got me through my time at the orphanage—Mercy's Light. Ironic name for a place that was a complete shithole.

There was a woman there named Mildred. She made us sit facing the wall if we so much as coughed. Lincoln and I used to count the seconds under our breath, just to remember what our voices sounded like. All that the lady wanted was quiet; if we made noise, it meant death.

I appreciated my foster parents, Peter and Maria Frost, because they took us out of the orphanage, but they had treated us like secrets that could never be spoken. I was sure they were only interested in collecting a check. They weren't especially attentive either; all we had was each other—Lincoln and me.

I stared back at George, wanting more answers. "Give it to me straight, George. Angela's missing, and I don't know how to find her. What's really going on in this town? Who's pulling the strings? How do my former foster parents factor into this? What game can this copycat Xmas Day Butcher be playing?"

He stayed quiet for a few moments, staring at the ground. I patiently waited for his answer.

"I don't know anything about your foster parents, but Doctor Thomas T. Tuttle and Mayor Carl Hamonte...Lenny, those are the names you need to remember. The doctor controls the institute. The other controls Whisper's Creek. The two of them together...they might control everything. Don't tell anyone I said that."

He slowly got up from his chair and looked longingly at the Christmas tree. "Clara's gone...Angela's gone...a return of a Xmas Day Butcher. Curse this damn town. This will not end well."

CHAPTER 8
DECEMBER 8TH

I found it near my front door in the early hours of the morning. The air was still frigid, and my world still felt empty—the days beginning to blur together in this frozen wasteland.

Another gift box, wrapped in shimmery red and green paper, miniature candy canes and gumdrops scattered throughout. I wondered what was inside this one. Maybe a body part? Something worse? I almost refused to check, horrified at what might lie inside.

I hesitated before touching it, my trembling hands lingering over the box. It was so quiet, so still in my neck of the woods. There were never any knocks or signs of the Xmas Day Butcher coming to drop them off. They were always just there—waiting for me—ominously. The only sound I heard was the faint creak of my floorboards as I stepped near it, a sharp ball of anxiety creeping up my throat.

I crouched beside it and lifted it; it didn't weigh much. I brought it inside as I shut my front door behind me. I placed it on my coffee table and just stared at it, hesitant to see what awaited me inside. After some deliberation, I ripped it open and lifted the lid to the box.

Inside was another red envelope. I tore it open and read the letter that was inside:

CLUE #4: *"Why did Clara go poof? In George's house—find your proof. Check her room, or you will hear of Angela's doom."*

The words were simple, but they felt like a blade being thrust inside my ribcage. "Doom." What was the letter insinuating? That George had something to do with Clara's disappearance all along?

My mind was spinning, trying to make sense of it. All the rumors in town...could they be true? Was George St. Nicklaus a secret murderer? Why did Angela need to suffer for all of this?

I stared at the letter for a long time. "Doom," the word echoed in my mind, but it just didn't make sense. I was so caught up in the idea of George being behind Clara's disappearance that I didn't notice the newspaper clipping that was also in the gift box, a second part to the clue.

I picked it up and read the headline: **CLARA ST. NICKLAUS MYSTERIOUSLY DISAPPEARS AFTER TOWN HALL XMAS PARTY.**

From what I remembered, Clara had disappeared after leaving the Town Hall Christmas party last year. No witnesses saw her after she left, and no camera footage had picked up where she might've gone. It was like she really vanished, out of thin air.

George being behind it never clicked in my mind because he was her father, for goodness' sake. But who else could it be? Sometimes the culprits hid in plain sight because they were too obvious to be guilty. But how did the Xmas Day Butcher know that George was involved? Is he just pinning it on him because he's the one who actually caused her to disappear?

So many questions...I couldn't take it. I was losing it. All I wanted was Angela back in my arms. I didn't want to play some sicko's twisted game.

I tried to keep a steady head and dialed Castillo's number before I blacked out again and did it anyway. I needed to talk to someone about this, someone who could potentially help me. Someone to pull me back from the edge of the cliff, to keep me from spiraling down into the hell that was my own mind.

She picked up after a couple of rings. Her voice, raspy from lack of sleep, cut through the blaring quiet in my house. "What happened, Lenny? Are you alright?"

I felt my throat tighten as I talked, the mounting fear strangling my chest. "There's another gift box, Detective Castillo. It had a note—it mentions George's house, and how proof of Clara's disappearance is there. He's threatening Angela's life as well."

I heard her sigh on the other end; she sounded irritated. "This Xmas Day Butcher is playing mind games with us, Lenny. We cleared George a year ago when she initially went missing. This guy's good at hiding who he is." Her voice was tense, and there was something about her tone—it sounded like she was on edge as well.

She let out a dry laugh. "This might be a stupid question, but you never considered any security cameras?" she asked, in a mocking tone.

I shook my head to myself. "I tried calling someone about that after the first 'gift,' but no luck in this weather. We never had the need for anything like that. This is all just insane."

I felt the weight of the letter in my hands as I slowly crushed it, anger tightening my chest. "Why me? That's what I don't understand. What did I do to deserve this?!" I shouted, infuriated.

Detective Castillo remained silent on the other end. I could almost hear Castillo thinking to herself, like she was trying to figure out what to say in a crazy situation such as this.

When she spoke again, her voice was quiet, sounding defeated. "Without any evidence on who this guy might be, we have to play the game. I'm sorry."

That just sounded like she was giving up because she had no idea what to do next. To be fair, neither did I. All I could do was follow the instructions of the letter.

The hairs on the back of my neck stood up as I slowly realized that I might be doomed, and that meant that Angela might be too. I was at the mercy of a madman.

I took several deep breaths, trying to calm myself, but it wasn't working. My jumbling thoughts came in and out like a revolving door.

Clara's face, the Christmas party a year ago, the way she had just...vanished. Just like Angela, from one day to the next.

No one saw anything—no footage, no witnesses. She just disappeared.

I shook my head, trying to push the thoughts away, but it was like a demon clinging to me. "I think George knows something," I said, my voice strained. I couldn't let it go. My gut told me I was right and that I needed to listen to the Xmas Day Butcher. There was something in his house, something I needed to find, and I knew something must've been there. Just like the reindeer earrings, it was a sign. "He's hiding something."

Castillo's voice became stern. It only made the pit in my stomach grow deeper. "Look, Lenny, Clara's disappearance is not on him. The Xmas Day Butcher is playing mind games with you. You want to know what I think? I think she ran away because she didn't want to be controlled by her father anymore. She was young and reckless, and she had her issues—maybe she just wanted out—forever."

She said that too easily, almost dismissively, but she may have had a point—maybe that's what had happened after all.

I didn't want to argue with her further; she wasn't going to be of any help. I appreciated Detective Castillo's efforts in trying to find Angela, but it just wasn't enough. If I was going to find her, I needed to do more—do things I normally wouldn't do. "Alright, Detective," I muttered sleepily. "I'm going to try and get some rest."

I hung up before she could reply. My words were a lie. I wasn't going to sleep—not now, not with this gnawing feeling in my stomach, urging me to follow the clue of the Xmas Day Butcher.

"I'm going to George's house," I said to no one in particular. "I need to see what he has hidden."

The thought of waiting and doing nothing was suffocating me; the growing unease in my heart because of Angela was never going to go away unless I found her.

I grabbed my coat off the lounge chair, sat in it, and slipped on my boots, which were resting beside it. I had no intention of calling

George to let him know I was coming; it wouldn't work. It needed to be a secret. I needed to go in and out to see what was really going on. I was a desperate man, and I was willing to do desperate things, even if it was a trap. I had no other choice.

When I stepped outside, the chilly air sliced my face. My heart raced at the thought of sneaking into George's house, but there was no turning back. I couldn't wait anymore. I needed to go.

But then—a voice spoke out to me: "*Come with me.*" I turned around, panic swelling in my gut; no one was there. All I saw was an empty land blanketed with snow.

"*Come with me!*" the voice growled angrily.

I couldn't tell if it was a manifestation of my mind or if it was someone in the woods taunting me from afar. I started to breathe rapidly, childish screams echoing in my mind, my head pounding with so much noise.

I ran back inside my house and shut the door just before I blacked out on the floor.

CHAPTER 9
DECEMBER 9TH

I jolted awake and immediately checked the date: **December 9th**. I had blacked out and slept through the day. I slipped my phone out of my pocket to see if I had made any calls; none were made.

I took in a few deep breaths and suspiciously eyed the interior of my house. It was quiet; except for the sound of cold winds rattling my windows. I hoped I hadn't done anything and that I had just slept. I checked my clothes—as far as I could tell, they were the same ones I had on the day before.

The screams had taken me back to the day they killed my family, and I couldn't handle it. I needed it to stop, and that's why I shut my eyes—closing my mind off to the world. Only the darkness calmed me.

Typically, I only blacked out during periods of highly stressful situations. Angela's abduction and the Xmas Day Butcher's evil game was breaking me in ways I didn't think possible.

I remembered my plan to search George's house for proof of Clara's disappearance—those were the words of the Xmas Day Butcher. I checked my watch again; it was **10:47 PM**. The town was engulfed in darkness, the perfect time to go.

Jesus, I was out for a long time, but I haven't been sleeping well at all lately.

I slowly rose from my chair, preparing to leave in the dead of night, when everything in George's house would be silent, including him. He was a heavy sleeper and went to bed early. I'd be able to sift through his house if I were quiet enough.

I had made the short trek to George's place and crept through his backyard, my breath fogging in the freezing air. I had the key to his back door firmly in my hand. I crouch-walked over to it and quietly inserted the key into the hole and turned it, slowly pushing the door open. It opened easier than I thought it would.

When I got inside, the house was very still. I crossed through the living room, careful not to make a sound. I went to Clara's bedroom first to search for the supposed proof.

I turned on my phone's flashlight and noticed that the room was very neat as I opened drawers and rifled through her clothes and makeup stuff—I didn't find anything out of the ordinary. I looked around, swiftly feeling my way around her closet, but there was nothing of interest inside.

I stared at her bed and crouched to illuminate anything that might've been underneath. I saw something. I crawled closer, and as I searched underneath her bed, I found an opened lock box with a red ribbon on top—similar to the ones I had been receiving at my doorstep.

How peculiar.

Inside, there were pictures of Clara with a guy I half-recognized. There were a few photos of them hugging at what looked like school events and one in a dark bedroom. I hammered my head for the name. Then it came to me—it was Henry Hamonte, Mayor Hamonte's son.

My heart skipped a beat. Clara never spoke much about Henry, but I sort of recalled them being friends. I had no idea that she was involved with him in an intimate fashion. It might've been something that was covered up. It was strange because...Henry was dead. The cause had been ruled as alcohol poisoning. A tragedy from approximately a year ago.

Why hadn't George told me about the connection with Henry and Clara? He was always so controlling of her. It really made me wonder—*did he kill her?*

I shook my head because I couldn't believe it.

Why would he?

I put the pictures back inside the lock box, shut it and slid it back under the bed. I needed to leave before George heard me.

I froze as the light clicked on in the bedroom. I was caught with my pants down, too lost in thought, not realizing he had woken up from his deep slumber.

I turned off the flashlight of my phone and stuffed it inside my pocket. I spun around slowly and stood up, without looking at him.

When I mustered up the courage to see him, he was standing in the doorway like a towering monster, his old, wrinkled face twisted with fury.

"I'm going to kill you, son," he growled, his voice low and dangerous. His thick, meaty hands were wrapped tightly around the handle of an axe.

My heart hammered in my chest. I hadn't expected to be caught like this. The anger in George's eyes was palpable, and I genuinely felt like he did want to kill me. Especially when he had that axe in his hands.

"Wait, just one second," I pleaded, backing up, my voice cracking. "George, please. I'm just trying to find out what happened with Clara. I know I shouldn't have broken into your house, but I didn't think you'd let me in here. I'm sorry."

George lowered his gaze, steadily staring at me, axe firmly in hand. He charged at me, knocking me down to the ground before I could move a muscle. *Thud!*

"*Gaaaahhh!*" I cried out in pain as my back smashed against the hardwood floor. He pressed the handle of the axe to my neck, both of my hands attempting to push it off, my arms burning with pain as he furiously pushed harder to choke me.

I sputtered, trying to regain my breath. "P-please...please, George," I squeaked out. "You're going to kill me." He saw my face turning red and froze. His arms grew weak as he slowly got off of me, guilt on his face, horrified at what he had done. He backed out of the room, staring at me as he did so.

I slowly tried to rise as my back flared; I was groaning and wheezing. As I breathed hard, my face was hot, my throat closed up, and my heart beat faster than I could count. "Holy shit, George. You almost killed me. I'm really sorry. I'll never come in here again without your permission." I dragged myself to the bed to leverage my body before I toppled over.

He lowered the axe and softened just a smidge. "You're right, you shouldn't be in here, you sly little rat. Look what you almost made me do!" He patiently came back in and took a deep breath. "Goddamn you, Lenny, if your wife wasn't missing, I'd beat your ass. You spooked me!" he shouted, looking around nervously. "I've been hearing things at night—footsteps, weird noises, like someone's been inside my house. I thought it was a fucking squirrel or something. It's been happening since the beginning of December. I thought I was going nuts."

Can it be the Xmas Day Butcher? Has he been sneaking in here? Did he leave the "clues" in his house? Am I being played?

I tried to steady my breathing as my heart pounded against my chest. "I'm really sorry, George. I didn't mean to spook you. I'm just looking for answers, okay? The Xmas Day Butcher left me another gift box. He says that Clara's connected to this."

George's eyes widened in shock as he set aside the axe by laying it against the wall. "Clara? Connected how?! What does that bastard know? What did he write to you?!" he demanded as he came closer.

I held up my hands, indicating I didn't know much. "He didn't say anything specific, just that proof of Clara disappearing is in your house. I don't know why. I think he's just playing games."

George tiredly rubbed his face and sighed. He sat down on the bed, defeated. "There's no damn proof of anything here."

I contemplated asking more, but I hesitated. The man had almost tried to kill me, but I had to—for Angela. I needed to know more. I needed to do what the Xmas Day Butcher wanted me to.

I quietly sat beside him and cleared my throat. "What do you think happened with Clara? Why do you think she's gone?"

George gave me an annoyed look and then scoffed. He cracked his knuckles and looked into space, misty-eyed. "I was strict with Clara because she liked to party and drink. She was only 22 years old." He sucked in a breath, fighting back tears. "We always fought about that. She loved her freedom and felt entitled to it, but I was trying to keep her safe. I loved my daughter, and I always will."

I nodded, understanding his reasoning. "So you were strict with her because you wanted to protect her?"

"Damn right," George said, his voice getting rough. "But when I found out she was seeing Henry Hamonte, that was it. That kid's nothing but trouble, and his father, the mayor—don't get me started on that crooked son of a bitch."

I swallowed hard, heat rising in my throat, the thrill of learning something new in this dark mystery. "Wait...you think Henry Hamonte killed her?"

George nodded firmly. "Oh, I'm sure of it. That boy was a disaster. I bet he killed Clara and hid her body somewhere. I always knew it was him," he muttered.

I took a deep breath. "It could explain why Henry is dead, too. He was found frozen in the snow just a few days after Clara's disappearance. They said it was alcohol poisoning."

George leaned in, turning his head, his eyes filled with fire. "You think that was an accident? That smells like guilt to me, Lenny. I bet he killed her and then did himself in because he couldn't take it."

It did make sense. If Henry was involved with Clara in a romantic way and things went sour, he might've killed her—perhaps by impulse or by accident. But he could never be properly questioned because he died soon after.

I rubbed my chin, thinking of any possible connections. "If Henry killed Clara, what does that have to do with Angela? What is the Xmas Day Butcher getting at?"

George shrugged. "Angela was at that Town Hall holiday party too, wasn't she? She worked for the mayor, after all. What if she saw something she shouldn't have? What if she knew too much? Remember—Mayor Hamonte is a corrupt little shit swallower. If I could crush him underneath my foot like a cockroach, I wouldn't hesitate."

I recalled what Angela had said to me once, before she vanished. She'd warned me that Mayor Hamonte wouldn't like the restoration project she was working on for Whisper's Creek, but she hadn't had a chance to give more details.

What if Angela's disappearance is tied to that restoration project? What if Mayor Hamonte didn't want that to happen?

There was a hard knock at the door. I froze. George looked at me, suspicion in his eyes. I could barely move, but I knew what it was. I had a feeling, churning away in my stomach.

We both slowly got up. George grabbed his axe as he led us down his dark hallway towards the front door. "If it's anyone I don't know, I might chop off their arm. I'm just letting you know," he warned.

When we arrived, he opened it slowly, and there it was, waiting for us on the doorstep. Another gift box, wrapped in white paper with a red ribbon.

George stepped outside and looked around to see if the person who dropped it off was still in the area. They weren't—they always vanished like a shadow.

I lifted it and opened it up. Inside was a red envelope, a bloodied Christmas gnome, and a severed finger with a ring on it. It was Angela's finger.

I glanced at George, my stomach rising with bile—his face paled. I kept it together and quickly tore open the envelope, sliding the letter out, reading it as George opened his mouth to say something.

CLUE #5: *"Do not trust him, but do check his basement; a man's secrets are grim. Check tomorrow night, and turn on the light. You'll see that the Xmas Day Butcher is right. Do not check before; I'll be at your door...I'm always watching you, Lenny, and always remember—Angela's body parts are plenty."*

I slowly looked up at George, my chest tightening with fear. My hands trembled as I stuffed the letter in my pocket. "What does it say? What the hell does it say?" he asked frantically.

"He cut off Angela's finger," I mumbled, my throat dry. "It's signed by the Xmas Day Butcher."

George gasped, short of breath. "My god..."

I have to play his sick, fucking game...I can't risk it. He'll kill Angela, or worse. Fuck! What the hell will I find in George's basement? When will this end?!

CHAPTER 10
DECEMBER 10TH

I couldn't stop shaking as I paced through my house, my hands trembling so hard that I dropped the latest gift box on the floor. The walls felt closer than usual, like they were suffocating me. George had kicked me out of his place; his horrified face had frozen with fear, ordering me to get out of his house like I was some stranger. The clock had struck midnight as I raced back home, freezing winds wrapping me in their unforgiving cold.

He wanted nothing to do with the madness surrounding the Xmas Day Butcher. He said it was complete nonsense, and he wanted no part of it.

But it wasn't nonsense. It was real.

I sat down in my chair, trying to calm down, trying to keep the room from spinning. Eerie voices whispered in my ear: "*Angela...she's gone. You know what you've done; there's nowhere to run...do not trust him...*"

My living room was dark, and silhouettes of bodies seemed to dance around me when I wasn't looking. They slid across the floorboards, jumped around the Christmas tree, and inched closer to me—like they wanted to swallow me up.

I ferociously rubbed my temples, trying to stop the brutal pounding in my cranium. I felt him taunting me—the Xmas Day Butcher. That monster wasn't just out there somewhere, playing their sinister game, toying and torturing my mind; they were with me, twirling me around their finger, unraveling the very last crumbs of sanity I had left.

I couldn't stop seeing Angela's severed finger, frozen and red. The Xmas Day Butcher had left it for me like a deranged trophy of what he had done to my poor wife. That horrific image was burned into the inside of my eyelids. When I shut my eyes, I imagined her face contorting in excruciating pain, the pleading sobs as tears ran down her flushed cheeks.

I wanted to hold her close, to tell her it would all be okay. When I found her, I knew nothing would ever be the same again, but that was fine. We'd get through it—together. I had the Xmas Day Butcher to thank for that.

Something shadowy moved outside the window across from me as I jerked my head up, eyes wide. I froze, my breath becoming quiet. When I blinked, the black shape was there again—a tall, crooked thing staring back at me with cold, dead eyes. I couldn't believe what I was looking at. I blinked again, and it was gone.

I'm imagining things...I'm imagining things...it wasn't real.

I thought about going to Detective Castillo, but the idea filled me with a dull sense of hopelessness. She wasn't able to recover any traces of DNA from the gift boxes I had given her, and she wasn't much help, even if she wanted to be. She just didn't have the resources.

Waiting for her to do something was a death sentence. I needed to find the answers myself. I needed to do what the Xmas Day Butcher wanted. That meant that I needed to check George's basement tonight, without him knowing.

There was something about him, something different. Maybe I was just imagining things, but it seemed like he was hiding something regarding Clara and Henry Hamonte. There must've been something there, but I didn't know what it was yet.

My eyelids felt heavy, and I had a hard time keeping them open. I got up from my chair too fast and felt dizzy. When I walked forward, I tripped over myself and fell to the ground. I groaned as I turned on my stomach, rubbing my spine as it burned with pain. I couldn't take the tiredness anymore—I shut my eyes, engulfing myself in total darkness.

I woke up with a jolt. I was still on the floor, a heaviness draped all over my body. My head was still pounding, though slightly. Then I remembered what I had to do, as I felt a sudden surge of heat on the back of my neck.

George's Basement.

I checked my watch; it was **11:05 PM**. I slid out my phone and checked my call log: no calls. It seemed like I was behaving myself.

I still had time to do what I needed to do. I rushed to my room and pulled clean clothes out of the closet. I took off my own, which were sweated in, and quickly slipped on the new ones, which included: my coat, a beanie, a pair of gloves, and sweatpants.

I took a deep breath and reminded myself that I was doing it for Angela. I walked out of my house calmly and shut the door behind me, locking it.

I set myself on the path back to George's house. I still had his set of keys, and I wouldn't think he'd have the energy to change all the locks in the house just to keep me out. I kept my head down and marched on, braving the cold winds that were picking up as I went forward.

❦❦❦❦❦ ❦❦❦❦❦

George's house looked dead quiet in the icy darkness. I slowed my walk as I approached it and kept my eyes peeled just in case he was crawling around. I avoided the front of his house altogether and snuck around back. I hopped over the wooden picket fence and crouched down.

I waited. There were no footsteps, no labored breathing. I was good to go. I stood up, maintaining my balance, and gently stepped forward, one foot in front of the other, until I reached the basement door.

I saw the heavy padlock dangling from it—old and rusted. I had the key, but if I didn't, I was sure I'd be able to break it open with a good swing from a sledgehammer I could get from the nearby shed.

No one ever really went down there, not even George. I took the keys out of my pocket and inserted the right one into the lock, gently turning it until it clicked open. I grabbed it and took it out, tossing it aside on the ground.

When I gently opened the door, the smell hit me first—a musty aroma of old copper and damp air. My stomach almost erupted, but I kept it down.

I went down the steps cautiously, taking out my phone to turn on the flashlight. The beam illuminated the inside, while my throat went dry. My heart raced as I mentally prepared myself for anything to jump out at me.

The basement was creepier than I remembered, the walls lined with old wooden shelves for tools, cobwebs draped all over them, and a few boxes filled with tools were thrown about.

When I approached the center of the basement, I saw it. A dark shape, dangling from the ceiling.

My first thought was a mannequin—some grotesque decoration from the Xmas Day Butcher, in an effort to scare the shit out of me and send another one of his twisted messages.

When I raised my flashlight, I saw that it was a horribly decayed body—a dead one. It was wrapped in strands of Christmas lights, half-frozen and zombified. My breath quickened, and my heart hammered against my ribs as I dared to step closer.

I shone the light on the face of the poor victim. Her dead eyes stared blankly back at me, her lips slightly parted.

It had a pink sweater on, with a name tag.

I staggered backwards, my breathing becoming quick and frantic, my head spinning, my phone slipping from my shaky hand. I couldn't believe what I was looking at.

It was Clara's dead body.

CHAPTER 11
DECEMBER 11TH

The clock struck midnight on my watch as my face went pale, my mouth and eyes wide with disbelief as I stared at Clara's hanging, lifeless body before me. My hands trembled at my sides as I struggled to grasp the shocking revelation unfolding in front of me. Every muscle in my body froze, my breath growing shallow, my mind unable to process the impossible truth that stormed around my head.

Another damn gift box waited underneath the dangling dead body, like an old ceiling lamp. It must've been Clue #6. I didn't want to go near it, and I didn't want to open it, but I had to. I slowly crawled over to it and yanked it towards me—not wanting to touch Clara's frozen body.

I grabbed my phone from the floor and held the light on the box as I tore it open with my free hand. I lifted the lid and found a red envelope along with a single photograph.

The note inside read:

CLUE #6: "*The man did a dirty deed. If you ever want to see Angela again, George St. Nicklaus must bleed.*"

My heart nearly stopped; the Xmas Day Butcher was insinuating that George had murdered Clara, his own daughter. I had considered it in theory, but...I didn't know what to think.

I picked up the photo and looked at it. Angela—bound with duct tape, eyes bloodshot and terrified. On the back, something was written:

"Remember the deadline: Christmas Day. Kill George, or Angela dies."

I shoved the photo and the note into my pocket, tossing the gift box aside.

I couldn't believe it—George killed Clara. But it didn't make sense the more I thought about it. How would the Xmas Day Butcher know? What did they have to gain by pinning Clara's murder on George? Where was the body hidden all this time? It couldn't have been in the basement...could it? Was I that blind? No...no, it couldn't be.

Her body would've rotted away a very long time ago. Someone had kept it ice-cold all this time to preserve it, but why?

I didn't know what to do. I couldn't go to Detective Castillo, and I sure as hell couldn't confront George with the morbid possibility that he had killed his daughter all along.

I didn't know if I had it in me to kill George, my own boss. He was grumpy, but he wasn't evil, unless he really did murder Clara.

Still, if I murdered a murderer, I'd still be considered a cold-blooded killer. I was never that type of person. I hated violence and always tried to avoid confrontation all my life. Lincoln had been the opposite. He didn't mind throwing a punch or six.

Angela helped mold me into a good person, despite the bloodshed I had lived through.

I had every reason to be a raving lunatic—a dark soul corrupted by the tragedy of my murdered family—but I wasn't. I was simple and reserved—a married man who worked on a farm. Now I was being ordered to kill a man, and if I didn't comply, that meant my wife's death.

There was a sound upstairs. My mind went blank, and my heart thundered like hell. Then—heavy footsteps. He was awake, and he was coming for me.

George St. Nicklaus would be down any second, and I'd be forced to make a bold choice. All I could do was think of my poor wife, Angela. She had no foot, no finger...who knew what else the devil incarnate had chopped off my wife?

"Shit!" I whispered fiercely. "I'm out of time."

He slowly came down the stairs, wild-eyed and angry, firmly grasping his axe. I backed away, turning off my flashlight and sliding my phone back into my pocket. He flipped on a light switch, and a dim light lit up the room.

His reddened, furious eyes stared into my soul, but they quickly tore off me as he saw Clara's dangling body. "Oh my—oh my god! What the fuck is that?! You motherfucker!" George clutched his chest, his breath starting to hiccup as he couldn't believe what he was seeing. "Y-y-y-y-you killed her," he gasped. "You killed Clara, my baby girl. All this time—you were the one!" he shouted at the top of his lungs, his voice echoing through the snow-covered fields outside his house.

I held my hands up, trying to prove my innocence. I had no idea what I was in for. "No, it wasn't me! It was the Xmas Day Butcher! He did this! I swear it!"

He viciously shook his head, not believing me. "No! You're a liar! You broke into her room...I knew there was a reason why. You wanted things to remind you of what you did, didn't you? You sick little rat! Murderer!" his voice cracked. "Now I know it wasn't Henry. Fuck! I got the wrong guy. I killed Henry for nothing. I thought...I thought I had done it for Clara. But it was you all along. You were the one who killed my daughter."

My throat closed up, trying to make sure I had heard that correctly. "Wait, you killed Henry?" I asked shakily. "I thought his death was an accident. I can't believe you killed the mayor's son."

It made sense why he hadn't mentioned Henry Hamonte in connection with Clara's disappearance. He killed him without a shred of evidence to justify it and didn't say anything out of guilt. That's what George's "dirty deed" was, and somehow, the Xmas Day Butcher knew about it.

Before I could say anything else, he lunged forward, violently grabbing my collar as I shoved him back. He blindly swung his axe, barely missing me by a hair.

He firmly grabbed the axe and crept forward, foaming at the mouth with rage. "Killer! Murderer! You will pay!" I refused to die in that moment. Angela needed me, and I needed her.

I found random objects on the floor and started throwing them at him: an old hose, a garden gnome, a set of extension cords, and a storage box filled with old files. He hit them aside, getting angrier by the second.

He yelled and charged at me, axe held high—I used Clara's body for cover, and he stopped, lowering the axe, suddenly staring at Clara's dead body, misty-eyed. "How could you, Lenny?! How could you?!"

I crouched down and picked up a stray hammer from a half-opened toolbox. "I didn't kill Clara!" He picked his axe back up. "Liar!" I stood up and threw the hammer at his face; he cried out in pain, shutting his eyes and lowering the axe again. With my body trembling all over, I sped over to him and kicked the axe out of his hand by aiming for the handle.

I picked it up swiftly and swallowed down the lump in my throat. He fluttered his eyes open, glaring at me with such anger; every fiber and cell in his body wanted me dead.

He roared and ran forward, his hands balled into tight fists, his face twisting with bestial rage. I did what I had to.

I swung the axe back and swung it forward, straight into his chest.

With a horrifying *crunch*—it sliced into him, creating a massive gash of red—blood spilled out as he gasped for breath, his mouth sputtering, his eyes rolling to the back of his head.

My hands shook uncontrollably as he fell backwards, his body hitting the ground with a strong thud. The axe stayed fixed into his body, crimson liquid pouring out of him and onto the floor. "Oh god, oh my god," I whispered shakily. "What have I done? What the hell have I done?"

I looked all around, my eyes darting in all directions. I needed to leave—I needed to get the hell out of there. That's when I noticed the window; it was slightly ajar. That's when I realized how the Xmas Day Butcher had entered. But I couldn't stay thinking about that; I needed to go. My adrenaline surged through my veins, lighting up every molecule in my body.

I ran up the steps, my shirt getting caught on a pointed edge on the wall, a protruding nail. I ripped it off and exited the basement. I closed the door and didn't bother with the lock. I ran for my life, the cold biting into my face, freezing up my throat, and burning my chest.

I'm sorry, George. I'm so sorry.

CHAPTER 12
DECEMBER 12TH

S now was falling around me, enveloping me in a blur of white and freezing cold air. My mouth let out ragged breaths, my lungs turning to ice, my throat closing up. I stumbled through what felt like a snowstorm, my legs becoming heavy, the thick crunch of snow pounding in my ears.

I soon felt it. I whirled around and saw it. A shadowy presence was watching me, the same one from before—a dark shape lurking ahead in the eye of the storm. I powered through, trying to be brave, trying to show the shadow I wasn't afraid of it, despite the horrid act I had committed.

I tried to scream at it, but my voice was swallowed up by the snow. My heart hammered as I marched on, but the landscape suddenly changed. The snow turned into gravel. It wasn't cold anymore; it was hot, and the change caused my body to erupt with chills.

I was in an old building. I thought it was a hospital or an institute—the walls were cracked and peeling. The windows around me were broken and hollow, staring back at me like empty voids. There was a flurry of people inside—dark figures moving through the blackness, their faces distorted, their bodies blurring with rapid movement.

When I blinked, I was in front of a house, my home. It was cold again. My eyes noticed the Christmas lights hanging from the roof, the lights flickering erratically. An inflatable snowman buzzed on the porch. It should've felt joyous and festive, but it didn't. Everything was wrong. Angela was gone, unable to enjoy Christmas.

There was screaming all around me, glass-shattering shrieks that penetrated my eardrums like sharp knives. I shut my eyes tightly and covered my ears, trying to drown it out.

When it finally stopped, I opened them and saw Clara's frozen, dead face in front of me. I let out a scream and stumbled back onto the snow.

I tried to move, but my body wouldn't obey me. My head started to grow heavy, my thoughts spinning in so many directions. Something flashed across my mind—the visceral image of an axe carved into George's body.

Then—I woke up in my bed.

I gasped for air, my chest heaving, my body slick with sweat. The morning light shined through the window, bright and blinding against my face. I checked my watch; it was **10:22 AM.**

It had to be a dream. It had to be. But the aching in my arms and the searing pain I felt in my legs told me otherwise. It told me I killed George St. Nicklaus with his axe. What if someone saw me running through the snow?

No, that's impossible. Practically no one lives around George, and it was the dead of night.

I was the only person who interacted with George on a semi-regular basis. I needed to get my story straight; I needed to stay innocent for Angela. I raised my hands; they were pale, with no blood on them. But to me, the blood was still there; it was invisible...because I became a murderer.

There was no turning back. The Xmas Day Butcher got what he wanted; he thrust me into his twisted game. As long as I got to see Angela again, I'd continue with the game. What other choice did I have? I had no life without my wife. Without her, it wasn't worth living.

I turned my head towards my nightstand and grabbed my phone slowly, my fingers shaking as I dialed Detective Castillo's phone number. The phone started to ring. When she answered, I tried to steady my voice before speaking.

"Hey, Lenny. How are you doing? Anything on Angela?"

"Detective, I think something happened to George. He's not answering his phone." I loathed lying, but I had no other choice. I had to clear myself of the brutal crime I had committed. I knew my guilt would overcome me eventually, but for now I'd play the part for Angela.

"Did you visit his home?"

I was afraid of myself because of how easy it felt, the sly words slipping out of my mouth like honey. "That's the thing, I went to knock on his door and everything. He just didn't answer. I don't know what's up with him."

Castillo paused for a moment. "It will have to be quick. I'll be there in ten to pick you up, and we'll head over together."

I got up from my bed quickly and dressed myself before second-guessing what I was doing. I didn't have time to think or to process anything. I had killed a man, my boss, in cold blood. Meanwhile, Clara's body was still hanging from the ceiling of his basement. It was the perfect setup.

When Castillo pulled in, she beeped for me to get in the car. She drove fast with lights and sirens, not saying a word. Snow was falling; the town outside the windows was a blur of white, with not many people in sight.

That was the effect of having a severed foot inside a stocking in the middle of the town square. People were afraid. The Xmas Day Butcher had returned from the dead. I was certain they thought that, because I thought the same thing.

When we arrived at George's house and got out of the car, you could feel it in the air. It was too quiet and too still. Something was very wrong. I knew what it was, but Detective Castillo was about to find out.

We went up the steps to the porch. Castillo pounded on the door and waited. There was nothing but silence.

She turned, a concerned look on her face. "Let's go around back." I followed her as she went back down and walked around the house, towards the basement. My chest tightened as we got closer.

She inspected the door. "There's no lock." Her eyes scanned around our immediate vicinity and eventually found the open lock on the floor. "Found it," she muttered.

She swung open the doors and stepped inside slowly. I followed from behind, careful to keep my distance, just in case. I waited for her reaction...she soon gasped and cursed under her breath.

I peeked over her shoulder and saw that Clara's dead body was still there, cold, lifeless, and continuing to decay. George was nearby, unmoving, in the same position I had left him in—the axe cruelly impaling him.

Castillo remained motionless. She didn't speak and didn't move for a good thirty seconds. "Holy mother of...my god, Lenny. Clara...she's there. After all this time...the poor girl is dead, and George...good grief. What is this mess? This horror show?" she whispered, in utter disbelief.

I couldn't answer. I couldn't even breathe. The sight of them—of Clara and George, father and daughter, both dead...murdered...was truly haunting. I knew that this vile, disturbing image would be burned into my already tormented mind for a long, long time.

It reminded me of when Colton Kilhouser had slaughtered my family. So much death, so much destruction, so much pain...and all for what?

"No...it can't be. George is dead, Detective. He was my friend. I can't believe he's dead," I said softly, tears rolling down my cheeks. She turned and pursed her lips together, offering her condolences quietly.

When Castillo inched forward, she noticed the empty gift box on the floor beside the dead bodies.

Her low voice broke the silence, still full of shock. "Was this the gift?" she asked quietly. "Two dead bodies? Is this the work of the Xmas Day Butcher?"

I couldn't look at her. A chill ran down my spine as I tried to calm myself. "I... I don't know," I lied, but even I didn't believe it. "I think the Xmas Day Butcher has really begun the sick game he's been wanting to play."

She narrowed her eyes, scanning the rest of the basement. "There's a big mess here, like there was an altercation. George must've tried to protect himself from an assailant." Her cautious eyes landed on me. They drifted to my arms, which had a few bruises I hadn't noticed before, but she didn't say a word.

Her suspicious gaze was alarming. The idea that I might've been involved with George and Clara's deaths could've crossed her mind. But I wasn't saying a word. From now on, I'd keep the Xmas Day Butcher's gifts to myself, unless I felt I'd be able to ask Detective Castillo to utilize her assistance.

She inspected me closely. "You should go home, Lenny. You look exhausted. I'll call someone to take you. Don't worry, I'll handle this," she said gently. "Merry fuckin' Christmas, Detective Castillo," she said in an exasperated tone.

I didn't say anything. I only nodded.

I didn't remember much after an officer arrived to take me back home. I blacked out, hoping to wash out the dark memory of what I had done.

When I stumbled back inside my house, the dreadful silence echoed in my ears. A delayed sense of panic wrapped itself around my throat. I figured it'd only be a matter of time until Detective Castillo found out what I did.

I collapsed on the couch; the weight of everything I had done was crashing down on me. I could feel the guilt mounting inside of me like a volcano waiting to erupt.

I'd murdered George. He had killed Henry Hamonte; that's what he had confessed to, but it didn't justify what I did. It never would.

If he didn't kill Clara—was it the Xmas Day Butcher? And why? How did that connect with Angela? With me?

I couldn't make sense of any of it. I didn't know what was real anymore. My nightmares were becoming more vivid, and those images were blurring with reality.

There was movement near the window. It was the shadowy figure; it was staring at me with wild eyes. It looked like me at first, then it shifted into Angela when I blinked. I sprang up from my couch, prepared to confront it, but when I moved forward, it was gone.

I collapsed back onto my couch, the room turning upside down as my eyelids grew heavy.

A familiar voice echoed in my ears: "*Find me in the old white church...come with me...come with me! Now!*"

My body went numb as I blacked out.

CHAPTER 13
DECEMBER 13TH

I woke with a gasp, lungs burning, chest locked tight like someone had locked a belt around my ribs. My heart slammed against the inside of my body, desperate to escape. I was blacking out almost every day now, unable to control myself. It reminded me of when Colton Kilhouser had killed my family—how I felt back then, in a cloudy haze, believing it was all a cruel nightmare and nothing more.

I pushed myself off the couch, my legs shaky; the silence of my house was loud without Angela. The floorboards groaned as I walked towards the window, peeking out at the frozen, white wasteland. I pressed a hand against the icy glass, trying to slow my breathing, but it didn't help. My thoughts were a chaotic mess—flashing images of the axe being thrust into George's body, Clara's body hanging like a haunted swing set, and the severed limbs that the Butcher had sent me.

It was all too much to bear.

A harsh knock at my door interrupted my jumbled mind. At first, I thought it was in my head, but then I heard footsteps walking away outside, the subtle crunch of snow being stepped on.

I gasped. *It's him.*

Every part of me screamed not to move, so I didn't. Fear took over, paralyzing me. I took a few deep breaths and calmed myself down. Then I forced my feet to carry me forward—they felt slow and heavy, like I was being pulled back by an invisible man.

I made it to the front door and turned the knob, pushing to open. That's when I saw it—another wrapped gift box.

It sat neatly on the floor, wrapped in green paper and sealed with Christmas tape. My gut twisted into knots. When would it end? I couldn't do it again. I couldn't stomach seeing another chopped-off limb or being ordered to murder someone.

But there it was—waiting. I couldn't just leave it there, so I crouched down, my hands shaking, and picked it up. I brought it inside and shut the door. I tore it open, and inside was a pair of red Christmas underwear.

It belonged to Angela.

For a moment, I saw her warm face. I could see her so clearly—her infectious laugh, that teasing smile as she'd held them up to me in the retail store. *"These are just for fun,"* she'd said, her voice low and velvety. The memory hit me hard because she wasn't with me, and I missed her dearly.

My stomach broiled as I realized that the Xmas Day Butcher had taken them off her; how embarrassing and humiliating that must've been for her. There wasn't anything he wouldn't do to toy with me. I was growing extremely sick of it.

The air grew heavy in my house as cold filled my lungs. The hairs on the back of my neck stood up as I noticed the red envelope inside the box. He never failed to send one. I took it out and tore it open. I didn't want to read it, but I had to. I needed to know what was next.

CLUE #7: *"Now that he's dead, sleep tight in your bed. We will now learn about my doctor. This one's a real shocker!"*

The words seeped into me like a poison spreading through my veins. My vision blurred, my throat tightened, and I swore I could hear faint whispering in the other rooms in my house—shadows dancing along the walls, messing with my mind.

I didn't know who he was talking about, but Doctor Thomas T. Tuttle did come to mind. He worked in the Gibraltar Institute. I wondered if there was a connection.

I stuffed the letter back into the box and tossed it aside with disdain. I was losing it. I knew I was. George's murder was getting to me, and the guilt was strangling me. The faint whispers never stopped. They grew louder, circling me like screeching ravens, torturing my very soul.

These words came clear, slithering through my ears: *"You know what you did... you know what you did..."*

I sprang up from my couch, heart pounding in my head, wild eyes darting between the voices that seemed to take shape on the shifting walls. The shadows took on faces—they were strangely twisted and human-like.

"Who are you, Lenny?" it whispered, the distorted voice sounding like my own. *"Do you know what you've become?"*

I wasn't sure; I didn't know what I had become. I was losing sense of myself and sense of what was going on. I screamed at nothing, in a panic—raw and desperate.

"Find me in the old white church...find me there..."

I freaked out as I shut my eyes, wanting it all to go away and to never come back. "Who are you?!" I shouted. "Why are you doing this to me?! Who the hell are you?!"

There was no answer. When I opened my eyes, the shadowy faces were gone. I felt like a damn lunatic, shouting at nothing.

What the hell is the matter with me?

Another knock disrupted my thoughts. This time, I quickly raced to my front door and checked the peephole. It was a familiar face.

"Lenny? You in there, man? It's Joseph."

It was Joseph Candela. The guy who worked in the building where Angela and Mayor Hamonte worked. The guy who seemed to be secretly in love with my missing wife.

I thought about ignoring him, but I figured it wouldn't hurt to have some company. It was better than talking to the walls and slowly losing all of my marbles.

I went to the door and opened it. He stood there, in what looked like a cozy brown jacket, snow clinging to his boots, his head tilting at me suspiciously. "You look like damn hell," he said. "You okay?"

"I'm fine," I lied.

He frowned. "You're not fine, man. Come on. You need a buddy to hang out with."

I crossed my arms. "Why do you say that?"

He let out a chuckle. "Dude, you called me. You told me about George, bro! Poor guy was murdered, and something about Clara's dead body being found?! This town is going to fucking hell! This Xmas Day Butcher has everyone freaking the hell out!" He leaned in closer. "Plus, Angela's still missing. I know you miss her, man. I'll keep you company until she returns."

Shit. I don't remember calling him. Me and my big mouth.

I didn't want to go with him, but the room felt smaller by the second, the air thick with the echo of my own jumbled thoughts. So I followed him out and shut the door behind me.

Joseph's truck smelled like rust and old coffee. He didn't talk much, just hummed to himself while the radio played a Christmas song. The snow outside was blanketing the town in white.

His tiny, one-story house sat at the edge of town, near some woods, not too far from where I lived. As we approached it, I noticed his porch light flickering in the distance. He parked up front, and we got out.

We marched to the door and jammed his key in. "Come on in, pal," he said.

The moment I stepped inside, I smelled it—damp wood and the residue of bad cologne. The place was a cluttered mess. Tools, cardboard boxes, old holiday decorations, and masks sat in the middle of his bare living room, which only housed an old, ripped-up couch and a TV set on a dusty stand.

It made sense—Joseph was single, never married, with no kids. I had my suspicions that he was a serial womanizer.

When I inspected his wall adjacent to the TV, he had dozens of masks hung on nails. They were all lined up—faces of Santa and snowmen and reindeer—all creepy-like, looking at me with suspicious eyes.

What the hell is that about?

Joseph grinned and pointed. "Noticed it, huh? I've been collecting these since last year. It creeps people out—I like doing that."

I tried to force a laugh, but my stomach turned. The air turned colder in here, and I could've sworn I heard it again—right behind my ear.

A gentle whisper.

"It's him. He's the Xmas Day Butcher."

My heart rate rocketed. I jerked myself around; no one was there.

There was another one: *"You know it's true."*

I glared at Joseph, who was adjusting a Santa mask on the wall. I remembered Colton Kilhouser, how he wore a Santa mask when he killed my family all those years ago. It was Joseph; it was always Joseph. I couldn't believe I'd never seen it.

The voices helped me realize the dark truth. He was obsessed with Angela and he was playing me. I couldn't believe I hadn't seen it before.

"Kill him. Kill him now."

I stared at him as he walked over to a table and pulled open a drawer. A stash of photographs were stuffed inside. He came back my way, my heart still racing, and showed me a few photos he had of Angela. They were taken in her office.

It didn't look like she knew they had been taken, like he had snapped photos of her in secret...like a sick pervert.

He glanced at me and laughed. "Don't look so serious, Lenny. They're funny! Right?"

"Kill him now!"

Before I could think about it further, I stepped forward and lunged. My arms wrapped around his neck as I threw him to the ground; the stack of photos exploding onto the floor.

He shouted, trying to tear me off him, but I was determined to stop the madness, once and for all. "What the hell, Lenny?!" he yelled. "Have you lost your damn mind?!"

"I know you have her. You have Angela. Tell me where Angela is," I said icily, like something had possessed me.

He wriggled and squirmed, trying to break free. "I don't know, man! Those pictures were just me goofing off! She knew about them! She knew! I swear!"

Suddenly, my mind went blank, and I blinked hard. The subtle whispers vanished, and it was silent again. I didn't understand what I was doing or why I was doing it.

I let go of him as he coughed hard, and scurried away from me. "I—I thought—"

"You thought what?!" his eyes flashed at me angrily. "That I'm your enemy, or something? Are you insane?"

I held up my hands in peace. "No, no! I don't know what overcame me. I'm sorry. I'm so sorry. I saw the photos and...I don't know."

He looked at me with skepticism, eyes wide, unforgiving. "Just get out of my house, please. I don't want to hang with you anymore."

I slowly got up and straightened myself out. I understood where he was coming from; I'd do the same if I were in his position. I couldn't believe that I allowed the voices to convince me that Joseph was the Xmas Day Butcher.

I was really losing it, and I needed to put my head on straight. I knew that I missed Angela, but there was no excuse to become an empty shell of my former self—a raving lunatic who lost his sanity.

I could barely look at Joseph as I made my way to the door, thoroughly ashamed of myself. "I'm sorry, Joseph. It won't happen again. I...I'm sorry. I'll walk home."

What the hell is happening to me?

CHAPTER 14
DECEMBER 14TH

I had been sleeping in my bed when Detective Castillo's call came early in the morning and woke me up, just as the sunlight bled through my blinds, flashing my closed eyes. I grabbed my phone from the nightstand as I rubbed the grittiness from my eyeballs. I stared at my ringing phone, concerned about what she might say.

Can you please come down to the station to answer a few questions? That'll be it for me. It'd be over.

I took a deep breath, answered it, and pressed it to my ear. "Hey, good morning."

She didn't waste any time. "Hey Lenny, I just wanted to provide you with an update on George St. Nicklaus' case. I know he was your employer and a friend of yours. I'm sure it was very traumatic seeing that gnarly scene, along with Clara...just despicable." She sighed. "Look, George didn't leave behind any indication that he could've been the Xmas Day Butcher," she said, her voice low and steady. "But I found something in his bedroom—a safe that I cracked open with another officer. There were several hundred-dollar bills wrapped with rubber bands, along with a confessional note inside."

A confession? I never would've guessed. "I understand, Detective. Are you allowed to tell me what it was?"

There was a pause, and for a second there, I thought she was going to say "no." "A lot of it was ramblings about how Mayor Hamonte is corrupt and how he's in league with Doctor Tuttle from the Gibraltar Institute." I swore that I felt her rolling her eyes through the screen. "But aside from that, he admitted to killing Henry Hamonte because he believed Henry was responsible for Clara's death."

That I already knew, so no new information for me. I was hoping for something relating to Angela or even Clara. "My goodness. That is absolutely horrible. What about Clara? Did he confess to killing her?"

Her breathing was heavy, thick with exhaustion. "Nothing about Clara. The body's being sent to the institute to be examined." I thought that was odd. "Looks like that case is about to be closed."

Why would they send a dead body to a mental wellness center? "Why is Clara's body being sent there?" I asked, suspicion present in my tone of voice. "We have a special procedure that we do in Whisper's Creek; it relates to Doctor Tuttle's expertise. That's all I'm legally allowed to say. I was told to provide you with an update, per Mayor Hamonte's orders."

I furrowed my eyebrows, not exactly believing what I was hearing. It sounded like George was right about Mayor Hamonte and Doctor Tuttle. There was something very wrong going on in Whisper's Creek. "Well, I appreciate that very much," I said gently. "Is there any update on the objects you took from me? The items from the gift boxes I was sent?"

There was nothing but silence. I already knew what the answer was. "No updates at this time. Roads are still blocked."

I frowned, defeated. Thirteen days had passed, and I still had no idea where Angela was being held. I wasn't even sure if she was still alive. "Okay, thank you for your help," I replied as my heart dropped.

"Mayor Hamonte wants to see you, Lenny. He regrets not being able to see you earlier due to other commitments. May I come pick you up in thirty minutes?"

I found it odd that he had not written to me or called me ever since Angela's disappearance. I found it even stranger that he wanted to talk to me now. I couldn't pass it up—I needed to hear what he wanted to say.

"Yes, I'll be ready."

Detective Castillo didn't say much as she drove me to Town Hall. She seemed on edge; something must've been preoccupying her. Perhaps seeing the dead bodies in the St. Nicklaus basement had shaken her to her core. I couldn't blame her. I was on high alert from the second I entered her cruiser. I felt that at any second, she'd accuse me of murdering George, and that meant I'd be royally screwed.

I was finally able to breathe a sigh of relief when she dropped me off. As I entered the building, I was hit with a cold wave of air. I walked along a long row of side offices across a shiny linoleum floor. It was all very government-like. This is where Angela worked.

The mayor's office was at the end of the hall. When I reached it, the huge double-sided wooden doors swung open. Mayor Hamonte towered over me, looking down at me with a fake smile. He was a tall, ghoulish-looking man with ice-cold blue eyes and a fading hairline, with only a few white strands hanging on for dear life.

"Come on in, Lenny. Good to see you. Sorry it took so long to speak with you. I do have a town to run." I sheepishly smiled as a strange mix of pine and antibacterial soap wafted through my nose as I stepped inside and sat on a comfy, plush chair.

The wood floors in his office gleamed brightly under the humming fluorescent lights, just adding to the unease I was feeling inside. I noticed the photo on his desk with his son, Henry. They were near a sunny beach, holding up their fishing catches—two salmon. I was sure that Mayor Hamonte dearly missed his son; at least now he had an answer—George had murdered him.

Mayor Hamonte took a seat behind his desk, his posture stiff, his grin tighter than his black suit. His eyes had a glint of evil. The words of a dead man echoed in my ears: *"He's corrupt...do not trust him."*

"It's such terrible business," he said, his voice insincere with pity. "Tragic, really. But at least I can rest easy knowing George St. Nicklaus was the monster behind my son's murder. I feel for Clara...all tangled up in that miserable mess." He leaned forward. "I know you worked for the man, but don't worry—we know you had nothing to do with the atrocity that took place. I know your mind is on Angela, but I assure you that Detective Castillo is doing all she can to find this depraved Xmas Day Butcher." He sighed heavily and stretched backward. "It's absolute madness, Lenny. A severed foot in the town square, a missing person reappearing—dead... an evil game being played right before Christmas. I swear—this town's cursed."

I raised my eyebrows in surprise; that caught my attention. "Well, yes, sir. I'd have to agree with you. I believe there's a conspiracy involving Clara and Angela...I think the Xmas Day Butcher has been involved all along. He's sent some "gifts," as I'm sure you know. I just hope they can be identified with some sort of DNA swab."

He nodded at me, half-listening. "Unfortunately, I don't think the police department in Whisper's Creek is able to accomplish that at this time, but we are actively trying to find Angela and the person responsible for her abduction."

Why does that sound like a whole lot of hot air?

I didn't know what else to say at the moment. "That is my hope as well."

Mayor Hamonte stood up and stretched his legs. He stared out his window, the one that gave a view of the town's square. "Angela's a brilliant woman. She is a person with an amazing mind—someone who looks toward the future of this town. Whisper's Creek owes her a debt, and we must repay it by finding her."

To me, that sounded like a man who had no idea what was going on. He seemed to be putting on a show to keep me and the town at ease. In reality, I was sure he was freaking out internally, not knowing what to do. Or, maybe it was something else entirely—a dark secret he was hiding. Maybe it had something to do with his supposed connection to Doctor Tuttle.

When I saw a framed photo on the wall of Mayor Hamonte with Angela, Clara, Henry, Joseph, and a few other residents, my mind wandered back to last December's Christmas party in the Town Hall—the one I had missed out on due to an illness.

I pointed at the photo. "Clara was there that night, wasn't she?" I asked.

He turned around, snapping his finger at me. "Yes, she was. It's such a shame. It was a fun night, but now, it's forever tainted by the memory of her disappearance followed by her mysterious death." He sat back down, the weight of his grief sagging his shoulders down. "No one knows what happened to the poor girl. She must've slipped out before the party ended. George believed that Henry did something to her, but that's not the case. Makes sense that he did it, just like how he killed my son. You know how he was—controlling, angry...so much hate in his heart."

I nodded slowly, not wanting to disagree with him outright. "Listen, Lenny—I'm planning on a press release detailing the formal investigation into the death of my son and Clara's. We'll be concluding that George murdered them both, due to his confession, but we wanted you to make a statement concerning his character, since you worked with him for quite a while. Is that alright?"

I thought it was a very strange ask, but then I realized that's why he wanted me to visit him in the first place. He wanted me to help him form a narrative that George had not only murdered Henry, but he had also murdered his own daughter, Clara, even if there wasn't any concrete evidence that supported that.

A ball of dread formed in my gut, telling me something was very off. The way Mayor Hamonte stared at me—he made it seem like I didn't have an option to say "no."

"I understand, Mayor, but what about George's murder?" I dared to ask. "Is the investigation still open on that?"

He nodded strongly. "Oh, absolutely. We still don't know who sunk that axe into him. It's a very messy, horrific situation all around, and we're trying to keep our ducks in order. I'll have an assistant visit you in your home in the coming weeks to prepare that statement." He stood up and stuck out his hand to be shaken.

I obliged him, even if I felt like he was a man who was completely full of shit. "Okay, that sounds good with me. Hopefully Angela has returned by then, and this Xmas Day Butcher has been apprehended."

Mayor Hamonte waved me off with a fake smile. "Thank you very much for your cooperation, Lenny." He walked around his desk and opened the door for me as I walked out. He quickly closed it. I didn't trust that guy one bit.

I wasn't planning on leaving just yet. I wanted to check Angela's office. I took a sharp right, down a short hall, and found the door that said: **ANGELA FROST**. I opened the door quietly and got inside, slowly shutting it.

The air inside was familiar; it smelled like a sweet aroma of flowers. That scent followed Angela everywhere, and I recognized it anywhere. I scanned around her office, and everything looked untouched. I wondered if Detective Castillo had even bothered to check anything.

As I looked at the framed picture of us on her desk, the past came rushing back. A joyous memory—one I was happy to remember.

She'd come bursting into our house three winters ago, her rosy cheeks red from the cold, a gust of snow and sweet perfume trailing behind her. Angela's dark eyes had that gleaming light in them—the kind that made you lose yourself in them.

"Lenny," she said, voice full of excitement. "I got the job. I'll be working with Mayor Hamonte. I'm going to make a difference."

I wrapped my arms around her tightly. "That's so wonderful, honey. Congratulations, Angela. You deserve it more than anyone."

She talked about reform and change—rebuilding Whisper's Creek into a thriving small town. I'd believed her, too. I wanted change, for things to be better; that's all people want.

Only weeks later, she'd sat across from me at our dinner table, shoulders slumped, her eyes tired. "The politics here..." she whispered, "It's filthy. The mayor plays it better than anyone; that's how he consolidated his power. But I won't stop pressing for change."

I came back to the present, now standing in her silent office, her words sounding ominous in my head.

I walked forward and brushed my fingers across her desk. The dust-covered wood was as cold as ice. Memories rushed in—her warm laugh, her sparkly eyes, and the soft hum of her favorite Christmas songs under her breath.

Then I saw it—directly behind her desk. A small, metal safe with a numeric passcode. I went around and examined it. I felt it all around before inputting the code I figured she'd use: **0905**. That was her birthday.

It clicked open. I pulled on the tiny latch and searched what was inside. There was only a single white envelope. I picked it up and slipped out a note that was inside; it hadn't been sealed yet.

It was a letter that had been addressed to the *Ethics Commission*. It was Angela's handwriting—neat and strongly worded. I couldn't believe what I was reading. She was accusing Mayor Hamonte of siphoning public funds—diverting money into his own salary and into the Gibraltar Institute. She found it suspicious that he hadn't been able to allocate funds for a restoration project that she wanted to implement for the town.

My eyes saw the date: **December 1st.**

That was the day she vanished. My mouth went dry. I whispered to no one, "What could this mean? Could Mayor Hamonte be behind her disappearance to silence her?"

Before I could think about it further, an ear-splitting scream shattered the calm outside. It was sharp and guttural, tearing through the winds like a knife.

I stumbled to the window and looked down at the town square. For a second, I couldn't process what I was seeing. I thought my eyes were deceiving me.

But there it was, swaying in the wind, tangled in a mess of Christmas lights—a body...with no head. Just a dark shape hanging from the streetlamp, as some folks gathered around to take photos, while others ran for their lives—screaming.

My stomach felt nauseous as I started to lose sensation in my legs. My eyelids became heavy as I felt myself slowly falling to the ground—the world turning pitch black.

CHAPTER 15
DECEMBER 15TH

People ran in every direction. Mrs. Bloomfield from the bakery stood frozen in her doorway, flour still on her apron, eyes huge as she clutched a rolling pin to her chest. Two teenagers stared at it in disbelief, wondering if it was "cool" or absolutely horrifying. A mob of mothers scurried away, screaming, holding on to their children.

I stood in front of it, darkness all around me, studying it. I was surely in a dream, but I couldn't move, and I couldn't speak. It was like someone else was controlling my body.

The headless body was wearing a doctor's white coat. It was a grotesque depiction of violence. A hanging corpse, wrapped in Christmas lights, with no head, while snow had already begun to crust all over it.

Mayor Hamonte came running out of the Town Hall building, his polished shoes almost slipping on the ice that had formed on the staircase of the building, his breath fogging in short, shallow bursts.

He stood beside me, freaking out.

"Thomas?" his voice was in complete disbelief. "Jesus Christ! Is that Thomas?! This is why he hasn't been answering my messages..."

The name was immediately familiar. I'd heard George say it, Doctor Thomas T. Tuttle; he belonged to the Gibraltar Institute. For whatever reason, he was dead, and his head had been chopped off. Undoubtedly the work of the Xmas Day Butcher.

I heard police sirens looming as blue and red strobes painted the falling snow. Across the plaza, Castillo's cruiser slid to a stop in the parking lot.

She leapt out, hair whipping around her face, and barked orders at the chaotic crowd. "Clear the area! Get inside now!" She efficiently cut through the mass of panicked people to get to us.

Suddenly, I felt a gift box at my feet as orders were shouted at me. "Lenny, get out of here now! It's not safe! Go home now!"

The noise was drowned out as I spotted **CLUE #8** scrawled on top of the gift box in those jagged letters that were so familiar to me. When I crouched down to grab it—a high-pitched scream ripped through my eardrums, yanking me out of the nightmare.

I gasped awake on my couch, the gift box cradled in my lap. I looked around my house to make sure I wasn't dreaming again. As far as I could tell, everything looked normal.

I had blacked out again, and I tried to remember what had happened. First, I checked my watch; it was **December 15th.** I had been taken to Mayor Hamonte's office...I then searched through Angela's office before seeing a headless body in the town square and blacking out.

I believed I had regained consciousness because I had been outside with the mayor and Detective Castillo. She had urged me to go home, and that was how I ended up running back home and finding yet another gift box on my front door.

I must've passed out from sheer exhaustion on the couch. I just wasn't getting enough sleep. George, Clara, Angela, the Xmas Day Butcher...all of these people were revolving in my mind—refusing to leave. It was taking a toll. I didn't know how much longer I could take it—my sanity was being sucked out of me, day by day, hour by hour...I wanted it to end.

I took a deep breath and ripped open the gift box—tearing off the lid with a renewed sense of anger and frustration at what was happening to me.

There was a red Santa hat, dirty and stained. A pointed yellow star, the kind that crowned a Christmas tree, its edges smeared with dried blood.

There was a red envelope; I knew the drill. I tore it open and read another obscure riddle:

CLUE #8: *"Learn of my deadly task; he only needed to ask."*

There was more tucked underneath, inside the box. There was an official sheet with the *Gibraltar Institute* letterhead. It was a cleanly typed document, and it looked very official. Doctor Thomas T. Tuttle's name was stamped at the bottom—alongside a square-shaped photo of his bowl-shaped bald head and his lean, bearded face with hollow eyes.

He looked like a doctor who fit the bill of being cuckoo.

The document read like a case study and a confession. It spoke of a patient: Colton Kilhouser. In summary, Doctor Tuttle was developing the genetic profile of serial killers because he wanted to know why killers became killers.

There was also evidence that he wanted to have a serial killer essentially do his bidding—for "experimentation purposes" and "scientific discovery."

He stated that he understood the controversies surrounding his secretive research, but that he planned to defy outspoken critics and professionals in similar medical fields of research. He wanted to "silence" them. The rest of the document was littered with redactions.

From what I could tell, no one knew what Doctor Tuttle was doing in the Gibraltar Institute—except for a few key individuals...such as Mayor Hamonte.

He chose Colton because of how he killed Peter, Maria and Lincoln Frost.

A chill ran down my spine. My brother, Lincoln. The very mention of his name made me convulse, bile rising through my stomach. Lincoln had been a constant in my life—we had gone through the wringer together. I wished we had both made it that day. Sometimes...I wished I had died with him.

We felt destined to stay connected, through all the tragedy, all the hardship...he should've been alive. It angered me for a very long time. I closed myself off, my heart turning into ice—until Angela came along. She was the light that cracked through the stone-like man I had become.

The wording on the document was so sterile, so analytically cold, and disturbing. This doctor was a monster, and why he had been doing this type of research at a mental wellness institute was absolutely beyond me.

It must've been the corruption and collusion that Mayor Hamonte and Doctor Tuttle were involved in. That must've been why Angela couldn't get funding for the restoration project. I reached into my pocket and pulled out Angela's letter to the *Ethics Commission*, much to my relief. I had kept it.

Some of the pieces were beginning to connect—this is what the Xmas Day Butcher wanted. I was starting to believe that Colton Kilhouser had been alive all along.

There was another document stapled to the one I was reading. It was a note that Doctor Tuttle had addressed to Colton. **"25 Days. 12 gifts. Kill your target, my son. Merry Christmas."**

The idea that Doctor Tuttle had used Colton as a living, human experiment was deeply troubling and deplorable. He had ordered him to kill a target, perhaps me? But Doctor Tuttle was dead—probably at the hands of Colton, who was somehow still alive.

My mind raced with endless possibilities. They could've faked Colton's death. But why? For Doctor Tuttle to use him like a lab rat?

Also what did Doctor Tuttle mean by 25 days and 12 gifts?

I rubbed my temples, my head hurting from all the insanity I was having to mull over. I still didn't understand why Colton had abducted Angela and why he was toying with me. If he was ordered to kill me, why didn't he go through with it?

Why was he making it long and painful? It felt deeply personal. He must've had a vendetta against me. Something that had been planned for a very long time.

Perhaps Colton blamed me for everything he suffered through. Who knew what Doctor Tuttle had done to him and for how long?

I folded the document and shoved it back inside the box. I set it down on the floor. As soon as I got up, I felt a vibration in my pocket; when I slid out my phone, it was like she'd been listening to me.

I wasn't sure how I felt about her at the moment. I didn't want to trust her, but there wasn't anyone else *to* trust. I was on my own. I decided that I'd only tell her about pieces of evidence that I felt she'd be able to help me with.

"Hello, Detective."

She spoke quickly and urgently, not wasting any time. "Someone has escaped the Gibraltar Institute. They are considered armed and extremely dangerous. This might be the Xmas Day Butcher we've been searching for. Lock your doors, stay inside, and don't open for anyone. Stay safe, Lenny." As soon as she hung up, I sprang off my couch and did as she instructed.

I was now certain that Colton Kilhouser was the escapee and that he had killed Doctor Tuttle.

CHAPTER 16
DECEMBER 16TH

I barely slept because I couldn't stop seeing the hanging body of Doctor Thomas T. Tuttle, or what was left of him anyway. His frozen corpse, his white coat soaked through with blood and snow, missing head and all.

I sat on the edge of my bed, staring blankly at the objects of **CLUE #8** on my dresser. The bloodied Santa hat, the bloodstained star. The letter:

"Learn of my deadly task, he only needed to ask."

What the hell did that mean? What were they referring to?

My stomach turned just thinking about it. Colton was a killer, and apparently, I was next.

The knock at the door came sharp and sudden.

I flinched, coming back to the present.

"Lenny?" a voice called. "It's Joseph. You in there? Let's talk, man."

I wiped my face, stood too fast, and stumbled to the door.

Joseph stood on the porch, cheeks red from the cold, snowflakes caught in his hair. He held a brown paper bag in one arm, a bottle of red wine swinging in the other.

"Hey man, let's just forget about what happened. I know you're going through hell, and this is probably the worst Christmas you'll ever have," he said. "I figured you could use a drink. Well, maybe more than one, and I won't let you drink it alone—*amigo*." He winked at me.

Without saying a word, I let him in. Not because I *wanted* his company, but because part of me was afraid to be alone. I didn't know if I could trust myself after what happened with George. I didn't know what I was becoming.

He hopped inside, unbothered by the mess. I hadn't bothered cleaning anything up since Angela's disappearance. Files and unopened mail thrown about on our central table, empty cups toppled over on the floor, dirty laundry hanging off of chairs—I was a complete disaster.

I took a quick whiff and gagged. My place smelled like wet rats and dirty socks. The hairs on the back of my neck stood up because of how ashamed I was.

Joseph dropped the bag on the kitchen counter. "Eggnog, *muy* delicious," he said, pulling out a half-gallon bottle. "With a little holiday spirit." He cackled as he poured half eggnog and half wine into two mugs he pulled from my cupboard.

He pushed a mug into my chest, forcing me to grab it. "You frickin' need this, my friend. With all the shit that's been going on—we're living in a damn horror movie!"

"Yeah, you're right. Thanks," I muttered.

He shoved my shoulder and nodded. "You're damn right I'm right! It's Christmas time! Why do we have people getting their heads chopped off and shit?! What the fuck is happening, bro?! Good excuse to have a drink, though." He chugged down his special Christmas concoction and quickly poured himself more.

I looked at him carefully, wondering how much he was going to drink. He caught my stare and shook his head. "No, no. Fuck you. Don't judge me. This butcher motherfucker might come slice my ass off and eat it like a ham. I'll enjoy myself until then."

I let out a dry chuckle. "Fair enough, Joseph."

We sat down on my couch and tried to enjoy our drinks, even with all the murderous chaos around us. At first, we talked about the town—how everything had flipped upside down. The Xmas Day Butcher, the fear, the way Whisper's Creek felt like it was unraveling thread by thread, primed to explode.

"I mean, George St. Nicklaus?" Joseph shook his head. "Never thought I'd say this, but I actually miss the crazy bastard. I can't believe he was murdered like that, bro, and then his daughter showing up like that next to him?! I mean—what the hell?!"

"Yeah," I replied, sipping my drink. "It's all going to shit, Joseph. Angela...still nowhere to be seen, nowhere to be found. I'm worried, man. I don't know if I'll ever find her."

Joseph nodded solemnly and poured more eggnog for me. "You deserve a break. You need to take it easy. This is all too much for one *amigo*."

I didn't answer and accepted the refill.

A few hours passed. The bottle was drained—mainly by Joseph. My tongue got heavier and the ache in my chest softened. The snowfall outside deepened, pressing snow into the windows.

Joseph leaned back on the couch, eyes glassy.

"You know," he slurred, "I always had a thing for Angela. Not just the looks—though damn, those didn't hurt. She's smart, so sharp, so hot, hot, hot! I used to find excuses to talk to her at the mayor's office."

My grip on the mug tightened.

"She flirted with me, man. I swear she did. One time, she touched my arm and laughed at something stupid I said. That laugh...man..."

He trailed off, smiling like he was remembering something precious.

Then he looked at me and said, "You think she got tired of you? Maybe she's in on this whole thing. Playing a Christmas game for shits and giggles. Like, what if she just got bored, y'know?"

The world slowed and I sobered up quickly.

"You think this is a game to her?" I asked, voice low and hollow.

Joseph raised a brow. "I dunno. People change, Lenny. She did let me take pictures of her in the office. I wish she took me up on the offer to go back to my place for a more...private shoot." He shrugged. "Maybe you didn't know her like you thought—"

I didn't let him finish. All I saw was red.

I launched across the room and tackled him into the center table—it cracked beneath us. Mugs shattered. Eggnog splashed across the floor like blood.

He tried to shove me off, but I grabbed him by the collar and slammed him against the floor.

"Take it back!" I shouted. "You don't get to talk about her like that!"

We tumbled again—crashing into the Christmas tree. Ornaments exploded, ceramic snowmen shattered, a string of lights snapped loose and sparked.

Joseph punched me in the ribs. I hit him in the mouth. Blood sprayed across the tinsel decorations, and then—my hands found his throat. I squeezed—hard.

He clawed at me, choking and kicking, his face turning blue.

I squeezed even harder, until he stopped moving. Until his arms went limp and his eyes went still. I let go and sat back. I breathed hard like an animal after a kill. A cold, howling silence filled the room.

My hands trembled as I looked at him—Joseph—no longer drunk, no longer breathing...no longer alive.

What the hell have I done?

I scrambled back, heart thundering. My mind sputtered. I was standing in a grave I'd dug with my own drunk rage. I had to move.

I sprang up and grabbed him by the legs—dragging him toward the back door, every inch of my body on fire. The snow outside greeted me—it fell heavily now, blanketing my path to the forest.

I pulled him into the woods behind my house through frozen branches and piled-up snow. My back screamed with every step. Then I ran back, boots soaked and heavy. I grabbed the shovel from the hallway closet and sprinted back.

I dug a spot in the ground as my heart pounded like hell. The cold was beginning to numb my limbs, but I had to keep digging.

When the hole was deep enough, I remembered the old abandoned church that sat on the other side of the woods. I contemplated taking him there instead, stuffing him inside some hole, never to be seen again.

It reminded me of my brother, Lincoln, and how he always told me that that place reminded him of Mercy's Light—the orphanage.

I chose not to go there, there wasn't any time. I rolled him in with no further hesitation, or pity.

Just dirt and snow covering his lifeless corpse.

I ran back, icicles stabbing my lungs. When I returned to the house, I stood in awe of the violent wreckage.

The Christmas tree had fallen, the decorations were ruined, and the floor was splattered with red wine that looked like blood.

If Angela were here, she'd have my head. Then I saw it—Joseph's wallet and keys on the table. I grabbed them and headed back out into the snow.

Joseph's truck started on the third try. I drove through the snow, headlights cutting through whiteness—his house was only seven minutes away.

I parked carefully in his driveway, walked up to the front door, and let myself in.

Inside, I tore the place apart. I opened drawers, flipped his mattress, and yanked open cabinets. Looking for evidence—proof—anything to justify what I'd done.

But there was nothing—no hidden letters, no racy pictures, no weapons, no sign of Angela.

Just a normal house—a sparsely furnished home with booze in the fridge and those damn masks. He was innocent, as far as I could tell.

I stared at the mess, my frozen hands numb, my throat raw with tension. I'd killed an innocent man. No one would believe it was an accident. I had done it again—I had killed someone. I had allowed the alcohol to suppress my judgement, and I had allowed him to drive me into a murderous rage.

I had to leave. I stepped back, my breath ragged. It'd take me twenty minutes to walk home, and I had to hurry—before anyone saw me—before the snow let up.

I've killed another man. What the hell is wrong with me?

CHAPTER 17
DECEMBER 17TH

I sat frozen, drifting in and out of consciousness, my back pressed against the cold stone of my fireplace, the crackling flames doing little to warm the dull ache inside me. I was trembling—not only from the chill, but from the weight of the guilt that was eating me alive.

I heard Angela's laugh echo in the air, and it soothed me, just for a moment. I remembered her soft touch and the way she would smile at me from across the room, like we shared a love where no one else mattered—only us.

God, how I missed her. She'd been taken so suddenly; it was such a mystery. It felt like a dream now. No, not even a dream—more like a nightmare I couldn't escape.

I closed my eyes, trying to shut it all out, but it was impossible. Her absence gnawed at me in the silence of the house.

Colton Kilhouser was out there. I could almost feel it—his eyes on me, lurking somewhere just beyond the edges of my vision. He'd escaped from the Gibraltar Institute, and now he was hunting me down—watching me. He'd already taken my foster parents. He'd killed Lincoln and Doctor Tuttle, too.

Who was next? Why was he doing this?

Maybe it was because he was one of us—an orphan from Mercy's Light. A foster child who'd been discarded, just like me. Maybe he was picking us off, one by one. Maybe that was his sick version of revenge, or maybe it was something worse.

"25 days and 12 gifts." What did that mean?

I felt my throat tighten. Colton was toying with me—torturing me like a cat playing with a mouse before it kills it.

But I had no choice. I couldn't move. I couldn't leave. I was paralyzed. Not physically, but mentally. I couldn't think straight. My mind kept spiraling back to what had happened—to the family I'd lost. I squeezed my eyes shut again, hoping to block it out.

I heard Lincoln's voice in my head—his words cutting through the haze of my overwhelming turmoil. *"Leave with me, leave with me, Lenny. We're going to die. We must stick together if we're going to survive."*

I'd been too scared—too damn afraid of doing anything.

I saw him for a moment in front of me and then banged my head against the stone of the fireplace, shutting my eyes tight. When I opened them again, Lincoln was gone.

I could still see it so clearly, the day he was killed by Colton. The dark blood, the way his body crumpled to the floor, the way his eyes went blank, staring at me, lifeless. It sliced my heart, cutting it in two.

"Help me, Lenny. Save me."

His final words hit me like a sucker punch to the gut. I could still hear the whispers of the dead clawing at the back of my mind. I'd always been too afraid to fight back—to save anyone. Now they were all gone.

I kept seeing it, over and over. Flashes of what I had done, the atrocities I had committed to appease the wishes of the Xmas Day Butcher.

Sinking the axe into George's body, killing Joseph in a drunken rage...what monster was I becoming? What would Angela think of me, at the end of it all?

I buried my face in my hands, sobbing. The horrors I had inflicted were overwhelming. I never wanted any of it. I never wanted any part in this sick game. I couldn't trust myself anymore. I didn't know who I was.

A brutal knock at the door snapped me out of my endless spiral.

I froze, heart slamming against my ribcage. Was it him? Was it Colton? He loved playing games with me. I could feel it. I was losing my mind. Was this real, or was I just imagining it?

The knock came again, louder this time.

I didn't want to move. I didn't want to face whatever nightmare was waiting outside. What if it were Detective Castillo? What if she knew what I had done? Was it all coming to an end? Would I be forced to do something I didn't want to do?

I pushed myself shakily off the floor and crept slowly to the front door. The house was still a damn mess. I shook my head, ashamed of myself.

My legs wobbled, and my heart pounded so hard in my chest I thought it might implode.

I lunged forward, eyes in the peephole. There was no one there. I looked downward. There was a box—another gift box. I opened the door, slid it inside and quickly shut it.

CLUE #9 was scrawled on top of it.

I snatched it up and ran back to where I was sitting, cradling it in my arms. It was wrapped in the exact same way as the others.

I couldn't breathe; I couldn't think. My hands were shaking as I ripped the wrapping paper and pried the lid open. Inside, nestled in the center of the box, was a dollhouse. A tiny replica of a house, down to the minute details.

I found that to be so odd, but I knew it meant something.

Beside it was a small, delicate doll dressed in a Christmas outfit. A figure very familiar to me.

A chill crept down my spine as I reached for the red envelope inside the box. I tore it open and read the letter.

CLUE #9: *"I work through the night, because the world is not right. You must do the same; remember, there's no shame. You've done it once; now do it twice. Kill the name that rhymes with Sam; let's have a dinner with some Ham."*

My stomach twisted at the thought. The written words felt like a noose tightening around my neck. I couldn't do it again. I was already going mad enough.

I can't kill someone else, I just can't...but Angela. I have to think of Angela. Oh god...what have I done to myself? What have I done to deserve this torture?

I knew exactly who they meant, and I had to do it. I had to obey, or else Angela would die.

I had to kill the mayor.

CHAPTER 18
DECEMBER 18TH

It kept me up all night, the moral dilemma of it all. I had no real justification for murdering George. Only that I was ordered to by a madman who had my wife. Someone seemed to be playing a long game of revenge.

I was outside—standing in front of the spot where I buried Joseph. Something truly took over me in that moment—a sudden darkness that moved my body, causing me to do an irreversible act of evil. I told myself that I had to do it, for Angela's sake. I had to play the game of the Xmas Day Butcher.

I crumpled the letter in my hand, my heart thudding painfully in my chest. I walked back home, snow falling all around me. I thought about the dollhouse and what it could mean. I used to play with a certain type of doll, and so did my brother. It had comforted us throughout our tragic upbringing.

We had them in Mercy's Light, but we always had to hide them from Mildred. She hated them—that cruel witch hated everything. I wondered...there was an older kid who lived with us. He hated our dolls as well. I forgot his name, but not his face. He had a scrunched-up face with dark eyes that looked like buttons and a mop of dark hair that rested over his forehead.

He didn't quite look like Colton Kilhouser, but people changed as they got older. I wondered where that older kid went after we left. Perhaps this Xmas Day Butcher was closer to me than I originally thought—maybe there was a grand reason for all of this murder and death. I just wanted it to end.

I tried to push the memory of what I had done to George and Joseph from my mind. The guilt was suffocating—absolutely unbearable. I needed to forget. I needed to move on. I couldn't imagine doing the same to Mayor Hamonte.

I thought about what to do next as I made it back home. I felt an overwhelming sense of exhaustion weighing me down, and I couldn't entirely trust my mental faculties anymore. As much as I didn't want to call for Detective Castillo's help, she seemed to be the only option.

As I kept mulling it over, I tried to tidy up as best I could. I swept up the broken pieces of glass and ornaments. I threw the Christmas tree over the cracked center table so it'd seem like it fell over. I picked up a few other things and tried to make the place seem semi-normal.

I planned on using the excuse of severe mental deterioration because of what was happening to me and the town. Most of it was true; I was just leaving out the part about getting into a fight with Joseph and killing him like a raging lunatic.

I grabbed my phone and dialed Castillo's number. The line clicked, rang a few times, then picked up.

"Lenny? How are you? How can I help?" her voice was tired and strained. I was sure that she had her hands busy with the escapee from the Gibraltar Institute, whom I believed to be Colton Kilhouser, somehow still alive.

"I need you. Please," I said, my voice hoarse. "Can you come to my house? It's important."

There was a long pause. "It's been insane, Lenny...with everything going on...I'll come by briefly. This town is going to hell."

"Thank you." I hung up, the weight of the decision already bearing down on me. I knew I shouldn't have been asking a damn detective for help. I knew there was a chance I'd incriminate myself. I just had to try my best to keep it calm and collected.

When Castillo arrived, she barely gave me a second look. She was all business, her gaze sharp as she entered the living room and scanned all around. My heartbeat was rapid as I tried to control my breathing.

"You don't need to worry about the escapee. Everything's under control," Castillo said sternly, but there was something in her voice that didn't sound entirely reassuring. "We've got most of our officers patrolling the outskirts of Whisper's Creek—on high alert. Mayor Hamonte gave the order himself. After what happened to Doctor Tuttle, he's not taking any chances. We have to find this person."

I nodded slowly. "Any officers keeping an eye on the town? I know there's not that many to begin with, but..." I trailed. "We have a sufficient force patrolling town, but Mayor Hamonte dictates our priorities."

That doesn't sound corrupt at all.

"Right," I muttered. I wasn't convinced. "Because whatever's been going on in the Gibraltar Institute takes top priority."

Castillo gave me a sharp look. "I follow the mayor's orders, Lenny. He believes this can be the Xmas Day Butcher. We find the escapee, we find your wife. Right? Now, what did you need from me? I need to go back on patrol soon."

I brought out the dollhouse I had received, and she turned her focus towards it. Her fingers hovered over it, but she didn't touch it. Her face remained neutral as she examined the piece with a keen eye. "This person is psychotic. Why the hell do they keep sending you such odd things?"

She glanced at me.

"Have you seen Joseph anywhere, by the way?" she asked.

I stiffened, my gut flaring. "No. Why? Is something wrong?"

Castillo hesitated, and I could see the frustration mounting on her creased forehead. "He didn't show up for work this morning," she said. "His truck's in his driveway, but there's no sign of him in his house, and someone ripped the place apart. I'm fearing the worst."

I froze. "Oh my god. Joseph? No...could it be the Xmas Day Butcher? Why would they take Joseph? This is very alarming."

Castillo's expression darkened. "I don't know. A neighbor said she saw a male figure going in and out of the place—figured it was Joseph, but it wasn't. This is becoming a circus. This town is being terrorized by one person, and we have no idea who they are. I wish we had more resources; it's not enough."

I ran a hand through my hair, pretending that frustration was bubbling up inside me. "What are we going to do about this? They're coming for us all."

Castillo didn't respond to that. Instead, she took a step back and surveyed the mess in my living room. The furniture looked like a tornado had ripped through it, and the remnants of some empty bottles were still scattered around the floor. The faint smell of alcohol and eggnog still lingered in the air.

Before she could make a comment, I filled the silence quickly. "It's been rough without Angela. I...I've been a drunk mess lately. Can't seem to get it together, you know? That's why my house doesn't look great. It's just this Butcher...he's been driving me absolutely insane."

She looked at me for a long moment, sighing, her eyes softening just a fraction. "I understand. I know it's not easy for you. These are the worst days of your life. Just don't get lost in it, Lenny. You're not alone in this. I'm trying my best to find this Xmas Day Butcher and your wife."

Castillo turned back to the dollhouse—her fingers finally brushed against the delicate figure, but she didn't pick it up. Instead, she nodded slowly to herself, her mind working as she processed the details.

"This..." she hesitated, her brow furrowing in thought. "This reminds me of a case I read about so many years ago, from a town called Axe's River. There was a serial killer there who left dolls beside his victims. I don't know if there's any correlation, but it comes to mind."

I raised an eyebrow and scoffed. "Great name for a town. We've got Whisper's Creek, Gravestone, Axe's River, and Deadman's Lake—all neighboring each other."

Castillo, who'd been observing it, raised her head and looked at me. "This killer in Axe's River had a very specific method," she said. "He'd butcher his victims and leave a creepy doll beside each one at the scene of the crime—that was his signature, a calling card. The locals started calling him the *Dollhouse Killer*." She paused, shaking her head. "This killer was never caught, and it's been years since he's killed anyone. It's possible that this is the same person. New town, new method. It's all I can think of." Castillo shifted her feet, her expression becoming more focused. "You think the Xmas Day Butcher might be the Dollhouse Killer under a new name?" I asked, shocked at the revelation of this mysterious killer in Axe's River.

"I think it's a possibility," Castillo said.

"Who did he kill?"

Castillo glanced at me, pausing for a moment. "Medical professionals, outspoken journalists...people of that nature."

That's what Doctor Tuttle must've used him for...to kill his rivals.

I raised my eyebrows in surprise. I wasn't expecting that at all. "So...Colton Kilhouser," I said, the words stuck in my throat, "is actually the Dollhouse Killer?"

Before Castillo could answer—the window exploded with a terrifying crash. Shards of glass flew across the room like shrapnel from a bomb, and something heavy landed on the floor with a sickening thud.

I could barely process what I was seeing at first. The severed, bloodied head of Doctor Tuttle was in the center of my living room, its vacant eyes staring up at me.

The head had on a Santa hat—an ominous note stuffed in its mouth.

"Not again," I muttered under my breath.

Castillo's eyes widened in disbelief, but she was already moving. "Stay here!" she ordered as she bolted outside, nearly smashing through the front door, not even waiting for me to respond.

I hesitated. My legs felt like they weighed fifty pounds, but I forced myself to move. My gaze shifted to the head, and I approached it carefully, almost afraid to touch it. The absurdity of it hit me all at once—*Doctor Tuttle's head*, in my living room, wearing a goddamn Christmas hat.

This Xmas Day Butcher has a fucked up sense of humor.

With nervous fingers, I pulled the note free from its mouth.

CLUE #10: *"Tell Detective Castillo that she'll never find me. When she dies, it will bring me so much glee!"*

I shuddered as I read it. This Xmas Day Butcher seemingly planned on killing everyone in town—everyone I knew, anyway. I feared that Mayor Hamonte and Detective Castillo were next on the chopping block.

I turned to look at her just as she returned, puffing and wide-eyed.

"He's threatening you now," I whispered, my voice barely audible.

For the first time since I had seen Detective Castillo, I saw raw fear in her eyes.

CHAPTER 19
DECEMBER 19TH

My nightmare unraveled in sharp flashes—rapid images stitched together at random.

A large, metal door creaked open.

Inside: the white, padded room was empty except for a motionless body beneath a thin white sheet. Alongside it was a creepy doll—with a cracked porcelain face and glassy, lifeless eyes.

When I blinked, a narrow, dark alleyway materialized, a thick fog surrounding it. A motionless figure with a shadowy face was slumped against a brick wall, a camera strap tangled around its red, slit-open neck—more than likely a journalist.

A doll is propped beside it, dressed in a tiny plaid shirt to match the victim's own. A photograph of the gruesome scene was held up by the doll's tiny arms—a terrifying display of evil.

When I blinked again, I saw a hotel door that hung broken from its hinges. I floated inside, overturned luggage and scattered papers littered the floor.

Half a body was sticking out, underneath the bed. A press pass splattered with blood sat beside two outstretched hands that had been severed. A dark red outline showed the violent butchering of the arms.

On the nightstand, a doll sat with its legs dangling over the edge, a newspaper clipping embedded in its torso.

The headline said: "**THE DOLLHOUSE KILLER STRIKES AGAIN.**"

A sudden darkness overtook my eyes, and the vision shifted to a hardwood table illuminated by a single flickering bulb overhead. Newspapers were spread out like evidence of a series of grisly, interconnected murders.

The papers floated in front of my eyes, showing me the various, shocking headlines:

"DOCTOR THOMAS T. TUTTLE — DISREGARDED AND DISRESPECTED BY THE MEDICAL RESEARCH COMMUNITY."

"5TH VICTIM DEAD IN STRING OF BIZARRE MURDERS. ALL HAD SPOKEN OUT AGAINST DR. TUTTLE. CONNECTION OR COINCIDENCE?"

"DOCTOR TUTTLE STRONGLY REFUTES ALL

CLAIMS THAT HE HAD HIS OUTSPOKEN CRIT-ICS—MURDERED."

"WHAT IS THE SECRETIVE, DARK HISTORY OF THE GIBRALTAR INSTITUTE?"

The papers started to flutter around each other—pages screaming and flying like a ferocious tornado. A stitched doll with glinting, red eyes flashed in front of me, making my heart drop.

Everything went black.

I woke up, heaving and panting, rubbing the sweat off my forehead—before it dripped down to my eyes. I scanned my bedroom—thankful that I was safe, for the time being.

I checked my watch, it was: **December 19th**.

I got up quickly and glided over to the kitchen. I needed something in my stomach—anything would've sufficed.

I had stayed behind after Castillo left. She had told me to keep my head down and to stay out of trouble. Her exact words were, "Don't move, Lenny. Stay put."

She carefully took Doctor Tuttle's head with her and the dollhouse. I didn't tell her about the letter he had left behind—my morbid instructions. I couldn't let them stop me. The only concern I had was Angela's life and what I had to do to preserve it.

I had been restless almost the whole night—thinking about this *Dollhouse Killer* and if they had a connection to the Xmas Day Butcher. I thought about how my brother and I had played with dolls in Mercy's Light. Someone had been watching us—someone had been keeping track of us. The more I thought about it, the more I believed that the Xmas Day Butcher was someone from my past—coming to destroy me.

Maybe it was Colton Kilhouser, or maybe it was someone else.

I decided to make myself a hot chocolate in my kitchen, something sweet in a futile attempt to calm my nerves.

I wrestled internally with the idea of having to kill Mayor Hamonte. I didn't even know how I'd be able to get close to him like that. It was madness. I contemplated telling Detective Castillo the entire dark truth, but that'd be the death of Angela and me.

I was stuck between a rock and a hard place. The Xmas Day Butcher had me cornered, and there was no getting out.

Castillo had mentioned that she needed to visit her mother after dropping off Doctor Tuttle's head and the dollhouse in evidence. She was worried about her after I'd told her about the threat against her life.

She said her mother was a bit frail and wanted to make sure that the Butcher wasn't going after her in an attempt to draw her out.

I was so sick and tired of staying home, the snow falling all around me, the white blur of nothingness blanketing the entire town. I hated remembering the horrid nightmares of the night before.

I wanted to get out of the house.

So, I left. I zipped up my coat, slipped on my boots, and left my home.

I trudged through the snow along Coldview Street—a one-way road that stretched outside the town square, towards Castillo's neighborhood. As I walked along the snow-lined path, I felt someone following me—watching me, but every time I turned around—I saw nothing.

I'm losing my damn mind.

Castillo's place was in the oldest part of Whisper's Creek, where the houses were wrapped in decaying porches, with old street lamps flickering the whole night. But to be fair, all the houses in Whisper's Creek were like that or beginning to look that way.

I knew I had arrived when I saw Castillo's police cruiser parked in the driveway of a one-story home, snow piled up on the rooftop.

Castillo's mother answered the door.

"Hi, Ms. Castillo," I said, giving her the softest smile I could manage. "Is everything alright? "

She squinted up at me, her voice dry. "Not really, but I'm not dying yet, so there's that."

She looked very much like her daughter, just older, shorter, and with a few more wrinkles.

I managed an awkward chuckle. "That's good to hear. What happened?"

She ushered me inside, letting out a heavy sigh. "Someone broke in and stole some documents from Juana." The house was dark except for the glow of a TV in the back bedroom. The place looked normal, but Castillo's desk near the front window told a different story.

There were drawers open and papers scattered. The place looked ransacked. "I'm sorry to hear that."

"She's in the back," Ms. Castillo said, shuffling toward the kitchen. "She's upset." Right on cue, she came out and looked at me in surprise. "Lenny? What are you doing here?"

I shrugged awkwardly. "I wanted to make sure you were alright. I see they broke in."

She came around and inspected her desk. "Yeah, they took some documents from me. It'll be fine. I'm just glad my mom's okay."

I nodded. "Right, of course."

My gaze stayed locked on the desk. "Did they take anything specific? Something classified, maybe?"

She waved a hand, not looking at me. "No, nothing like that."

I stepped closer. She was acting suspiciously, like they *had* taken something specific—something she didn't want to get out.

What are you hiding, Castillo?

Before I could think further on the situation, the front window *exploded.* Glass flew in our direction like razors. I ducked on instinct, covering my head and face. Castillo and her mother screamed at the top of their lungs.

An axe wrapped in Christmas lights had buried itself in the wall beside Castillo's desk.

I just stared at it, breath frozen in my chest. Then I saw it—taped to the axe's handle, a piece of folded paper, fluttering slightly from the wind that had come in.

I crawled towards it slowly and pulled it loose, heart beating in my ears.

"Don't you pout; it's all coming out. Lenny, may I ask, have you figured out what this is all about?"

I didn't have time to process it as a surge of anger erupted in me. I shoved the note into my pocket and bolted out the front door; Castillo ran out alongside me. We were met with nothing but snow and an empty neighborhood. I jogged ahead, trying to see if anyone was around—nothing. There was absolutely no one.

"Do you see anything?" she asked.

"No," I whispered. "You? " I asked, glancing back at her.

She shook her head furiously. *"We're chasing a fucking ghost!"* Her eyes swept across the darkened neighborhood, wild and unfocused. "This evil fuck is always one step ahead. I don't know how. They're always watching. They know too much. How? How do they know so much?" she mumbled to herself.

She was beginning to lose it too; her resolve was cracking.

I stared into the darkness and saw nothing.

"When will this end?" I whispered.

CHAPTER 20
DECEMBER 20TH

Detective Castillo was irate after what happened in her home. She rushed me home and told me to stay put—that it wasn't safe to go outside. I could tell that she had no idea what to do—I didn't either, even though I had been ordered to kill Mayor Hamonte.

Another night of restlessness. I woke up after only a few hours of sleep, thinking and mulling over how it was all going to end. I thought about Detective Castillo and what she might've been hiding. Was she interwoven in the web of corruption that included Mayor Hamonte and Doctor Tuttle? That was yet to be seen.

My phone buzzed and I checked it. It was a text message from Castillo: *"Someone broke into Mayor Hamonte's car last night, we're still assessing the damage. Extra patrols are being posted at his home. Stay safe and out of sight."*

I sat on the edge of my bed, the lights off, only flashes of the red-and-green strands of light on the axe still glowing faintly in my mind. Things were getting crazy out there. If the Xmas Day Butcher was bold enough to break into the mayor's car—there wasn't anything he wouldn't do to get what he wanted.

I thought about the first time I had learned of the man who had killed my family: Colton Kilhouser.

It was Corita who told me. She was the old Spanish woman who took me in after that horrible tragedy. She used to feed me sweet bread dipped in hot milk; her wrinkled hands were strong despite her old age, and she was a woman with a big heart.

She lived in a small, cottage-style home with one bedroom. I slept in the living room, on an inflatable mattress, and kept my clothes in a closet adjacent to the bathroom. It wasn't ideal, but I wasn't complaining. All I thought about was trying to live my life in peace.

One night, after I woke up screaming—same nightmare, same screams she'd heard for weeks—she sat beside me on the mattress and whispered the truth.

"*El hombre malo, Colton Kilhouser,*" she said. "*Él lastimó a tu familia, mi amor. Él los mató. Dios no lo perdonará.*"

"That bad man, Colton Kilhouser," she echoed. "He hurt your family, my love. He killed them. God will not forgive him."

The evil man in the nightmares I experienced looked like a reflection of myself, killing my family. When the bullies in school would echo that same idea, I began to think that I really was the one who had killed them, and that Colton Kilhouser was just a boogeyman, a myth, a fall guy.

That name haunted me for so many years. Even when Corita delivered the news that he had died, I still felt his dark presence, casting a shadow on my life. It turned out I was right, that he was still alive somehow. Doctor Tuttle had been using him in the Gibraltar Institute, and it seemed like Colton had finally escaped.

That sweet old lady, Corita, had passed away years earlier, but I never forgot the way she told me that Colton Kilhouser had killed my family. She told me like it was a lie—something to shut me up and to never bring it up again. That idea lingered in my head ever so often.

I snapped back to reality and got up to stretch my legs. The house felt so quiet and frozen. I thought I heard whispers of someone coming, but I knew I was being paranoid.

I walked to the window in my room and stared out at the snowfall—it never seemed to end. I wondered how the Xmas Day Butcher was able to drop off gifts, severed heads, axes, and notes, all while remaining undetected and unseen. He was like a force of nature, not to be trifled with.

I imagined him out there—in the forest near my house, likely locked up somewhere with Angela, biding his time while he carried out his long game of vengeance.

The snowfall reminded me of the time when I lived in Mercy's Light with Lincoln. My mind went back to those days of misery...

The long, boring days that bled into each other in that dreadful place, black and cold. I spent most of my time staring at the scratched-up wall, the one that looked like someone had been clawing at it—like a ferocious animal. Not because I was curious about it, but because I didn't want to get into any trouble.

Mildred, the head caretaker, didn't like noise. She didn't like coughing, crying, laughing, or talking—especially not from Lincoln and me.

Her brutal hand was always quick to redden my cheek.

Our only solace was in the far corner of our living quarters—a dollhouse, dusty and broken. It had a few tiny beds inside with tiny dolls. We pretended to live there, pretended like it was our alternate reality—where we hadn't left our home, and our parents were still alive.

I remembered the way Lincoln and I used to sit on the dust-filled floor together. We'd huddle by the cracked window to try and catch a glimpse of the outside world—to see if we could attain any shred of joy from anything we might've seen.

The only thing we ever saw was the scorching hot sun, or the snowfall blanketing the town.

Lincoln's favorite dolls were the damaged ones—ripped-up things with missing buttons and made-up stories on what they had gone through. Lincoln's stories were always the most violent. It mirrored the horrors of what we had seen while living in downtrodden places, bouncing from one broken home to the next, while our parents fled the criminals they had stolen from.

That was about as much as I cared to remember.

He held his doll up, examining it. "Do you ever think we'll get adopted?" he asked, his voice carried that tone of careful hope. We knew we had to temper our expectations, when it came to the kind of lives we wanted to live.

"I don't know," I said. "It's quieter when it's just us, anyway. I don't miss all the screaming and the fighting. It scares me."

He smiled at that, a sad smile. "I know. I don't miss it either."

Then a shadow loomed over us. A taller kid—older, broad-shouldered, mean-mugged, molded by the cruelty of Mercy's Light.

I tried to remember his name. Colton? I thought it might've been Colton. To me, it fit his face somehow.

He sneered down at us. "Stop playing with dolls like girls," he commanded. "Hand 'em over. I want them for myself. I'm gonna burn them."

Lincoln stood up before I could pull him back. "No," he shot back, chin raised up, not afraid of the older bully. "Go away. You leave us alone. We're not doing anything to you. Got it?"

The bully's face flashed with rage as he shoved him back, hard. Lincoln pushed back, harder. Suddenly, they were on each other, fists swinging, feet kicking across the dirty wooden floor. I wanted to step in, but it all happened too fast for me to react.

"Enough!"

Mildred's voice cracked through the room like a thunder bolt. She marched in angrily—long, gray, checkered dress, scornful eyes, that permanent scowl carved deep into her wrinkled, old face. She grabbed them both by the arms and yanked them apart.

"Insolent boys. You will learn to behave! You two in separate corners. Eight hours. No food, no water, no talking, no sleeping," she hissed. "Break my rules and you'll be broken instead."

Lincoln glared at the floor, breathing hard. Even then, I knew something had shifted in him. That was the day he started fighting everyone and everything, the day he stopped trying to stay quiet—his resolve had been broken.

He lashed out at the world after that. I was the polar opposite, but he was my brother. I loved him and I missed him more than anything.

When he was murdered...I never healed from that. I didn't know how. I still didn't.

I snapped back to the present and walked over to my couch, heat rushing to my face. My heart hammered in my ears.

Colton must've been there in Mercy's Light. The older bully might've been him. That's how he knew who I was, and where I was.

Colton Kilhouser had to be the *Dollhouse Killer*, but something didn't make sense.

Why change his name? Why go by the Xmas Day Butcher? Why abduct Angela?

What the hell did I have to do with any of it?

My phone vibrated, and I quickly slid it out. I received an email, and the subject line was: *POST OFFICE—item available for pickup.* An anonymous sender, of course, something that didn't seem traceable. I waited until the next day after I received it because they were closed.

What did the Xmas Day Butcher have in store for me now?

CHAPTER 21
DECEMBER 21ST

I t was **December 21st**.

I was running out of time. I had no choice; I had to go see what it had in store for me. I grabbed my coat and braved the furious, icy winds.

Outside, the town was swallowed in snow. The air seemed to glow with it, snowflakes drifting sideways in the wind, soft and endless. The streets were nearly empty; even the usual hum of traffic seemed buried under the white snow. Everyone was terrified to come out of their homes because of the Xmas Day Butcher.

As I crossed into the town square, I noticed **MISSING PER-SONS** posters of Joseph Candela and Angela stapled on wood posts and taped to street crossings. A knot grew in my throat, but I swallowed it down.

I kept my head down as I walked, the cold freezing my face off.

The post office sat at the edge of Hollow Oaks Avenue, its lights dim behind frosted windows. Inside, the warm air was refreshing. The clerk's window was closed; a small sign read *"Out for lunch."* I didn't wait. I went straight to my postbox to see what was there.

The key turned with a squeal. Inside, against the dull metal, sat a single red envelope. Beneath it, a small pig ornament—pink and round, wearing a miniature Santa hat. Its porcelain body gleamed faintly in the light.

A strange chill crawled through me. I reached in and took them both out. The pig was heavier than it looked, the cold seeping into my fingers. I set it on the counter beside me, and for a moment, it looked alive—its tiny black eyes reflecting the light like wet ink.

The envelope was unmarked except for my name: *Lenny Frost.* The handwriting was sharp, deliberate. I tore the flap open. A single sheet of paper slid out, crisp and white.

CLUE #11: *"He's a pig that's round like a mound, with a dark secret that's yet to be found. This is not a game. Kill him now."*

Beneath that, the address to Town Hall, with a small key.

For a moment, I stood frozen, the letter trembling slightly in my hands. I glanced back at the pig. It seemed to be mocking me with an evil smirk—glaring at me with cold, black eyes.

I knew what I had to do—I couldn't delay it anymore.

I had to kill Mayor Hamonte, or else I'd pay the price—Angela's life. I'd killed George and Joseph; now I was about to kill one more. I never imagined myself doing evil acts of savagery, but when you're thrust into a truly despicable game with no sense of morality, you find yourself doing anything to save the ones you love.

I folded the letter, slid it into my coat, and picked up the pig—examining it.

I did the only thing I could—I set out to kill Mayor Hamonte.

CHAPTER 22
DECEMBER 22ND

I waited in the dark across from Town Hall, my breath clouding the cold night air. I was prepared with a small, foldable knife in my back pocket. My plan was to find his dark secret in his office—lure him in with a phone call, and kill him.

Bat-shit insane? Yes. But, I was running out of time. Angela's life was on the line.

The street lamps cast long shadows over the building, but I stayed hidden behind a cluster of bushes—watching. Then, finally, the black SUV pulled away from the curb. Mayor Hamonte climbed inside and disappeared into the night.

I didn't waste a second. I circled the building, heart hammering. A janitor's door on the side was cracked open—left ajar, either by accident or careless habit. Quiet as a ghost, I slipped inside.

The corridors were dim and smelled of cleaning chemicals and old carpet. I moved as silently as I could, sticking to the shadows, edging toward the mayor's office.

As I neared, a door down the hall creaked open. A janitor stepped out, a mop bucket trailing behind him. He froze when he saw me, eyes narrowing. "Hey. What are you doing here so late? That's twice already I've seen you."

Twice? What is he talking about?

I kept my voice calm and steady. "Right. I forgot a document in Mayor Hamonte's office. I needed to grab it before morning. It has to do with a witness statement regarding an important police matter. I can't say anything else about that."

His gaze was skeptical. "Is that so? I don't remember hearing anything about anyone being authorized to be here at this time. Security usually patrols at this hour, but everything's crazy because of this Xmas Day Butcher psycho. I might have to call someone, just to check."

I caught his eyes, trying to show him I wasn't lying. "No, wait. It's...it's also related to Joseph Candela's disappearance. Detective Castillo is involved—she's been helping me with my missing wife, Angela. I need that document for her. It's a whole thing, trust me."

Something shifted in his expression, his shoulders relaxed. "Oh god, that's right. You're the guy with the missing wife. This Xmas Day Butcher is freaking insane, man. I can't believe someone like that is out there. I hope you find your wife, and I hope Joseph is found...alive. Be safe, man. It's getting crazy out there."

I nodded, appreciating the sympathy. "Thanks. You too."

He gave me a quick once-over. "Alright, just be quick, and don't get caught, his office is open because I'm cleaning. I don't like that guy anyway, to be honest. He's shady." He leaned in. "I never saw you. That goes for both times."

Both times? Was I here before? Why don't I remember?

I nodded and slipped past him, heart still racing, and moved toward the mayor's office. I reached the heavy wooden door and pressed down on the metallic handle; it clicked open as I pushed myself inside.

The rich smell of leather from his chair and the faint residue of cigar smoke hung in the air. His desk was cluttered—papers scattered, a half-empty coffee cup, pens sprawled toward the edge of the table, but my eyes locked onto a small safe inserted into the wall, behind his desk.

I went over quickly, and inserted the key I had been sent. I turned it and it clicked open. There were many folders and files stuffed inside, but one folded print-out caught my eye.

I pulled it out. It had a sticky note on it that said: *"A dark secret that's yet to be found..."*

I hesitated for just a moment, then carefully unfolded it.

It was a series of text messages between **HENRY** and **CLARA**.

HENRY: What are you even talking about?

CLARA: Your dad tried to force himself on me!! He's a creep!!!

HENRY: No way...he wouldn't do that.

CLARA: He did do it!! I need to tell someone about this!! He's the mayor!! It's NOT okay!! I would never lie to you.

HENRY: He's the mayor...and my dad...who's going to believe you?

This never made it on the news—it looked like a cover-up.

The words hit me like a punch to the gut. I searched the safe again and found photographs—I flipped through them. Pictures of Mayor Hamonte and Clara together at the Christmas party last year, Hamonte looked intoxicated—Clara seemed uncomfortable.

I could hardly breathe. This meant that Hamonte must've had something to do with Clara's disappearance...and her death.

A soft creak behind me made my heart leap.

Mayor Hamonte stood in the doorway, casually leaning against the frame, phone in hand, texting like he'd just come back to get something he'd forgotten. "I forgot my wallet," he said without looking up. "I wanted to order a Christmas ham dinner."

His eyes found mine, calm but sharp. "Hello there, Lenny. What are you doing in my office? You weren't invited."

I remained calm, remembering my task and what I had to do. "I know what you did." I waved the print-out and the photos in the air. "You're the one who killed Clara last Christmas."

He scoffed at me, like I'd said the most unbelievable thing ever. "You think I had something to do with Clara's death? Are you on something? I understand your panicked state of mind, with the anguish of your wife still missing and all, but this is absurd." His voice was even, almost bored. "You're obviously wrong. It was George. George snapped—he's the one who did it. He confessed to it—case closed."

I swallowed hard, the weight of everything settling in my chest. Mayor Hamonte had killed Clara and had covered it up; it had to be the truth. George St. Nicklaus killed Henry, but not his daughter.

What else was Mayor Hamonte hiding? I already knew he had a disturbing connection with Doctor Tuttle and the Gibraltar Institute.

"The evidence is here! Clara told your son via text message that you forced yourself on her! It's all here! The photos...everything!"

He clucked his tongue and scoffed. "So, you're the one who stole the key to my safe, huh? Someone broke into my car recently and now it seems—I know the culprit. I shouldn't be surprised."

I shook my head. "No. It wasn't me. I didn't break into your car. I had no reason to."

He glared at me with cold, hard eyes. "Then who did?"

It had been the Xmas Day Butcher, he broke into his car—stole the key to his safe and planted the evidence in the safe.

I stepped closer, trying to keep my voice steady. "Where's Angela? Where is she? She was working hard to get the Whisper's Creek restoration project funded, but you were diverting those funds—to your salary, to the Gibraltar Institute. What about your friendship with Doctor Tuttle? What was going on with Colton Kilhouser? You have a lot to answer for. I know you're connected to all of this. All of the lies and the secrets in this town—it all leads back to you."

His smile twisted while he sent a message on his phone. "I'm the one in charge, Lenny. I decide what's best for this town. I don't have to answer to anyone. Not you. Not Angela. Not that fool—Tuttle. You'll see."

My heart pounded with rage in my chest. "Do you have anything to do with Angela going missing? Don't lie to me, you piece of shit," I snarled.

His eyes flashed with anger. "No. I do not. I'd watch your tone, if I were you."

I pulled out the small blade I'd been carrying—steady in my hand. "This is for Angela."

Then his phone buzzed loudly. I glanced down, heart pounding. "You don't want to do this, son. Castillo will be here any minute. We can talk about this, in a mature manner—no one needs to get hurt. I can give you what you want, and you can give me what I want."

I breathed in short, hard bursts of air. "Oh yeah? What's that?"

"Your silence, Lenny. We can't have this town delving into chaos. All the rumors about Clara and what may or may not have happened need to be put to rest. I must remain mayor of this town, it's for the best. Trust me." He stuck out his hand calmly. "I know you won't do anything to me, it'd be suicide—face it. Only reason this place hasn't been swarmed with officers is because they're out trying to find this Xmas Day Butcher. I have every man and woman on the job. I am committed to keeping this town safe, for everyone."

I scoffed. "I can't believe you."

He laughed at me, like I was nothing, like I was a cobweb collecting dust in the corner of his office. "Believe it, Lenny. I know I'll be able to count on you when it comes to what I asked you to do—regarding

George and Clara. It's for the best." He smiled, thinking that he was going to get exactly what he wanted.

No way.

Panic surged through me, but it was too late. I had to finish what I had set out to do. There was no going back.

Every muscle tensed up in my body as I lunged—sticking the knife in his left eye, a volley of terror screamed out of him. Blood poured all over my hands as I twisted and sank it deeper into his skull—ensuring he would die.

I kept it there as he gasped and choked for breath. A few seconds later, he went limp as his right eye rolled back. I yanked the knife out of his socket and made my escape by opening the window to his office and jumping out, nearly blowing out both of my knees.

I used the adrenaline that was coursing through my legs before it dissipated—aiming for the forest so that no one would see me or the blood stained all over me.

I ran as fast as I could, disappearing into the darkness.

CHAPTER 23
DECEMBER 23RD

Detective Castillo had texted me: "*Call me when you can.*" I replied with a "thumbs up emoji." I had no intention of responding to her.

I found a gift box on the front door of my house as my watch struck midnight. I couldn't stay long at all. I grabbed it and ran back into the forest, like a wild animal—streaked with blood after killing its prey.

I found a spot in the snow and collapsed—exhausted both physically and mentally from everything that had happened. I had killed George, Joseph, and Mayor Hamonte. I had become a monster.

I stared at my blood-soaked hands and shuddered.

What have you done to me?

I tore open the gift box and found the red envelope, tearing it open. It said: **CLUE #12:** "*You're almost there, release the pain you've been forced to bear. Find the truth of them all, all of my pretty little dolls.*"

Inside the box were photos and official documents that were spilled out like evidence of a cover-up: victims posed beside painted dolls, a female officer's old photo, and a younger me with Lincoln, my brother, grinning like we owned the world. Old police records, stamped: **"CONFIDENTIAL."**

I couldn't believe what I was reading. The records explained how Colton Kilhouser had killed my family: Peter, Maria and Lincoln Frost. He had been admitted into the Gibraltar Institute and "died" due to an accident. The files were signed by Detective Castillo and stamped by Councilman Hamonte.

It explained how Doctor Thomas T. Tuttle orchestrated Colton Kilhouser's death to use him and mold him into a killer for his own nefarious purposes: to kill his rivals, critics, medical professionals, and journalists who had spoken out against him and his research methods.

Colton had "died", but only to the public. In the institute, he was still alive, being used and manipulated by Doctor Tuttle. After so many years, the truth had been unveiled. All the pieces were fitting together.

Doctor Tuttle molded Colton into the *Dollhouse Killer.*

That threw my mind into a whirlwind of emotions. I had been lied to all along.

Inside the box, there was a small empty dollhouse as well, and across its roof someone had scrawled in red: "*You will become me.*"

As I sat on the snow-covered ground, hopelessly alone and afraid, faced with the darkest moment of my entire life, I allowed the truth to uncover itself in my mind.

They tricked me—manipulated me into believing that Colton Kilhouser had died all those years ago.

Doctor Tuttle used him like a puppet to do his bidding. Colton had most likely had enough, and that's why he was terrorizing the town...but why me? What had I done to Colton to warrant all of this madness?

I'd soon find out. I needed more answers, but I couldn't move. I was utterly destroyed, my body in a state of complete fatigue. I tried my best to keep my eyes open, but I failed. I soon drifted into a deep sleep.

I was suddenly in my old living room on Christmas Day, standing near the dead bodies of my foster parents, Peter and Maria Frost. The dark figure in the red coat and the plastic Santa mask was nowhere to be seen.

The boy standing in front of me looked like myself, he was holding a bloodied pointed star. He was breathing heavily, his Christmas pajamas streaked with blood. I felt nauseous as my vision grew hazy, bile rising from my stomach.

Wait...am I Colton Kilhouser? All of my blackouts...it makes sense, even if I don't want it to.

I couldn't believe what I'd done. I truly didn't think I was capable.

It was all coming back to me now, the traumatic memory I had blocked out for so many years—the altered, manipulated scene that had been instilled and ingrained in my head by the adults that were around me in the aftermath of the tragedy.

Tears ran down my face as I faced an inevitable truth: my life was over. "Why me? Why?! Why would I do this?!" I screamed at myself.

The boy dropped the pointed star and looked at me with misty eyes. "I...I don't know. I got mad and...I'm a monster. Come with me, Lenny. Come with me. We have to leave. The police will be here any second. We can protect each other."

I shook my head and stepped back, fear strangling my chest. "No, I can't. Look what you've done. You killed them!"

The boy ran his fingers through his hair, not believing what he had just done. "Please, Lenny. We didn't mean to. All we wanted were the dolls. They never gave them to us. They always kept us locked away. We snapped...we couldn't take it anymore. I'm sorry."

He tried to step forward, but I screamed at him. I didn't know who I was anymore. I didn't regard myself as human after that moment of darkness. "I'm sorry. I don't even know who I am anymore. I hate you. I hate you!" I shouted.

He was taken aback by that and fell to the ground, his legs becoming weak. "We'll remember this, Lenny. We'll remember."

I jerked awake, my head hitting the snow on the ground. As my eyes fluttered open, I was still surrounded by the dark. I thought about what I had just dreamed before I'd forget it. That was the voice I had been hearing all this time, my own voice.

I knew why I was exacting revenge. I was punishing myself for what I had done...20 years ago.

CHAPTER 24
CHRISTMAS EVE

I quietly walked home to find Detective Castillo already there. I saw her inside my house, through the back window. She seemed to be searching for evidence of something—perhaps wrongdoing, or foul play.

I snuck towards the back of my house and entered quietly, pushing the door slowly, using the howl of the wind to mask the noise. I tiptoed to the living room where she was standing, sifting through my couch cushions.

She slowly turned her head and examined me from head to toe. She noticed how horrid I looked, covered in blood and ice. "Lenny...what..." before she could finish that sentence, I yelled and dove into her—tackling her to the ground and catching her by surprise.

I pinned her down with my body and pulled out her service weapon—aiming it at her like a deranged lunatic. Her eyes were large and full of fear, her hands in the air, her mouth shaking.

"M-Mayor Ham is dead. It was you," she whispered, her voice was trembling. "You killed him and you killed George. Didn't you? Joseph too? Angela? What have you been up to, Lenny? What have you done?"

I got off of her slowly, keeping the gun pointed at her. She started to get up. "No!" I commanded. "You will stay on the ground and you will tell me the whole truth—all of it!"

She gulped and took a deep breath. "What are you talking about?"

I shook the gun angrily at her. "You know what I'm talking about!" I boomed.

She rubbed her forehead and scoffed, probably at the absurdity of the situation. "I should've known this was coming. All this time...the chickens have come home to roost."

"Yes they have," I declared.

"Lenny, cops are out there—looking for you. We know you were in Town Hall, in the mayor's office. We know you killed him. We questioned the janitor you spoke to and Mayor Hamonte texted me just before you murdered him. You don't have a lot of time."

It was true, I didn't have a lot of time left at all—it was Christmas Eve. I still didn't know where Angela was, but at least I was finally getting some answers.

"Do you know why I murdered him? I think you do."

She glanced at me, her shoulders slumped—defeated. It was all coming apart, all the lies, all the deceit, all the dark secrets that had Whisper's Creek in a stranglehold.

She took in a deep breath and blew it out. "Mayor Hamonte tried to force himself on Clara at the Christmas party last year, when they were alone. She was going to out him, and that would've derailed his career. So he ordered me to kill her and to cover it up."

I gasped, utterly shocked at her admission of guilt. "You're a monster! You killed an innocent girl! You deserve the same fate as Hamonte!"

She glanced at me with solemn eyes. "I know. I've done many bad things for Mayor Hamonte and for Doctor Tuttle."

"You don't know what you've truly done, detective. You were involved in faking Colton Kilhouser's death so that Doctor Tuttle could use him for his own evil purposes. Guess what? You helped create a monster...and he's come back to haunt us all."

She looked away, eyes downcast, unable to face me. "I know."

"Why? Why did you do it?" I asked, stunned that she would do such a thing.

"Do you know what they told me?" Castillo said. "They said if I helped, they'd make sure that my mother received the medical care she so desperately needed. They said if I didn't, they'd ruin me. I chose my mother. She was very ill and I couldn't cover the bills. I did it for her."

"You should've told the truth sooner," I demanded. "Why didn't you tell me that I'm Colton Kilhouser? That I'm the Dollhouse Killer?"

She widened her eyes at me—confused, shocked...so many emotions erupting out of her face at one time. "You're not Colton Kilhouser."

I tried containing the ferocious anger building in my chest, it felt like a ball of fire was expanding in my stomach and would explode at any moment. I was sick of all the lies.

I crept closer as I pointed the gun at her, trying to steady my aim. "Tell me the goddamn truth."

Tears flowed down her cheeks as she held her hands higher in the air. "I am telling you the truth. I swear. You're not Colton Kilhouser."

She was lying. Why? I wasn't sure. There could've been no one else. I was the one blacking out, not remembering the things I'd been doing. I was sure that I was the one, destroying myself from the inside out.

"Then who is?!"

She shut her eyes. "If I tell you...you'll kill me."

"Who is it?"

"*Kill her*", a soft voice rang out.

"What?" I questioned aloud.

"*Kill her now.*"

I looked straight into her eyes as she opened them. She remained quiet. I aimed the gun at her head and pulled the trigger—a single bullet ripping through her head. Her body clumped to the floor—a pool of dark blood spilling out of the hole in her skull.

I dropped the gun, horrified at what I had done. I walked to her still body slowly, to inspect it. She was dead, and there wasn't anything I could do about it. I went to my front door, opened it and surveyed the area—to see if anyone had heard the gunshot. I saw no one yet.

But there it was, another gift box. I kicked it inside and shut the door. I stared at it with such rage that I tore it open like a hungry animal tearing his prey to shreds. There was a pair of bloodied reindeer earrings inside, along with a red envelope. I opened it and read the letter:

"*Merry Christmas Eve. The end is nigh. Find me in the old white church. I urge you to do your worst. Come at midnight...it's time to make it all right.*"

CHAPTER 25
CHRISTMAS DAY

I took the gun with me and waited in the forest, like a wild animal. I stared at my watch, waiting for the clock to strike midnight. When it'd be Christmas Day. A few minutes later, in the cold, unforgiving darkness—the clock struck midnight.

I got up, my legs sore, my body aching, my head pounding...but I marched on, through the snow, using the trees as leverage to keep myself up. I knew that this was the end, but I didn't care. I had been forever changed, and I knew the person responsible.

After all of these horrible, traumatic days—after all of the people I had murdered in cold blood...I knew the truth, I only needed to confirm it. Everything I had blocked out, in my mind, concerning the dark truth surrounding my family's massacre—would come to light.

I had to face it, after 20 years.

I had no other choice.

After a good while of stalking forward, braving the howling winds that seemed to slice at my face—I walked through an opening, out of the forest, that led to an open, snow-covered field.

There it was—the abandoned white church. It sat quietly in the heavy winter snow. Its white paint was faded, blending in with the world around it. Snow piled up against the cracked wooden doors, and icicles hung from the roof. The windows were broken and covered in frost. A leaning tower stood tall and strong, a giant wooden cross coated in ice.

I dared to walk over to it, my heart pounding in my ears. When I reached the entrance, I took a deep, cold breath. I pushed open the heavy doors as they screeched and whined.

When I stepped inside, layers of snow covered the empty, dusted floor and the long abandoned pews. It was dark and quiet inside. As I walked forward quietly, the sounds of my footsteps echoed over the massive overhead arch of the building.

Stained, decorative panes of glass reflected the specks of moonlight creeping in. I didn't see him at first, but when my eyes adjusted to the darkness—there he was. A lone, shadowy figure at the end of the great hall, standing in front of a headless ceramic statute, a sharp, curved weapon in hand.

I pulled out the gun and kept it at my side—prepared for the worst. As I got closer, I saw a half-frozen, zombified man, who looked just like me. It was like staring into a dark mirror. I gasped and stopped dead in my tracks.

I couldn't believe it—I didn't want to believe it, but it was the dark, horrible truth.

The man stepped forward, the light from the moon illuminating his face more clearly. He was dressed in all black—a tattered sweatshirt clung tightly around his thin frame, and ripped cargo pants hung loose around his legs. The half-torn boots he had on seemed to fuse with his veiny, frosted feet—his frozen toes peeking out of them.

"Hello brother," he said in a haunting voice.

I gasped quietly, that voice—it brought back so many memories. I already knew who it was. It was unmistakable. My gut felt like it had an iron belt constricting it, crushing me so hard the air was being sucked out of me.

"Lincoln...it's you. You're alive."

It was my twin brother.

After so many years of believing he was dead...he wasn't, he was alive—standing in front of me, like an undead corpse from our dark past.

He nodded slowly. "I've been playing a long game of revenge, brother."

I shuddered, a cold spear rushing down my spine, my limbs trembling...I couldn't believe it. Lincoln, my twin brother, had been the one.

He abducted Angela—to exact revenge on me.

"Why? Why do all of this? Why...why abduct Angela? Why mutilate her? Why, Lincoln? Why?" I asked softly, confused as to why my own brother wanted to torment me with such a horribly twisted game.

Lincoln rose the hatchet in his hand and pointed it at me angrily. "Because you abandoned me! All those years ago! I know the truth."

I shook my head, not sure what he was referring to. "What are you talking about?"

Lincoln rested the hatchet on his shoulder. "When I...killed our foster parents. I asked you to come with me. You didn't listen. We could've protected each other—while on the run from the police. We could've met here. I told you, the abandoned white church, but no...you left me to die!"

I remembered it all. The memories I had blocked out, what had truly happened that day—20 years ago. I now knew the truth. Colton Kilhouser was my brother, Lincoln Frost.

He was the one who had murdered our foster parents. My mind conjured a dark figure to explain the events that had been told to me—over and over again.

That Colton Kilhouser had killed my family and that Lincoln was dead. Colton never existed, it was a name—an alias...to hide the tragic truth.

The voice I had been hearing was his, all along. Fragments of my shattered memory coming back to haunt me.

"I'm sorry, Lincoln. You killed our foster parents. I was terrified of you. I'm so sorry. I couldn't leave with you that day."

Lincoln paced back and forth, fury apparent on his darkened face. "Do you know what they did to me? Do you understand it? He faked my death, named me Colton Kilhouser—to mold me into his own personal serial killer."

My breath came up short, guilt burning in my stomach. "Doctor Tuttle?"

He nodded. "He was fascinated with the minds of serial killers—that sick bastard. Doctor Tuttle would order me to leave and kill targets he deemed dispensable—like his rivals, and the people who criticized him. I always left painted dolls where I killed my victims. The doctor deemed it incredible how I was never caught." He paused for a moment, shutting his eyes, most likely remembering all the people he had killed. "The newspapers started calling me the *Dollhouse Killer*."

It all made sense—the pieces were fitting together. Colton Kilhouser was the killer alias that my brother used, the one that was forced upon him. In a way, Lincoln Frost still died that fateful day—a dangerous serial killer born in his place.

"Why would they fake your death? Why choose you?"

He scoffed at me, shaking his head. "I was a young boy, who killed...Doctor Tuttle nurtured me into a serial killer from a young age. He told me it was right—to lash out at a world that hated me. Tuttle funded all of Hamonte's campaigns, so that's how I ended up in his grimy hands. He convinced me that no one ever loved me. From bouncing around foreign countries, to Mercy's Light, to our foster home...no one ever wanted us. I listened to him, because he was the only person I had—because you left me behind, and betrayed me."

I couldn't believe how Doctor Tuttle had manipulated my brother's mind, it was sickening. He molded him into a serial killer for his own disturbing motives.

"How did you do all of this? The gifts at my door? Clara's body in George's basement? The game you've been playing...you were like a shadow."

"I had a lot of time to plan. I knew it all because Tuttle told me everything, over so many years. He knew about Clara's cover-up, Mayor Hamonte's secrets—how he controlled the Whisper's Creek police department." He sighed heavily, the burden of it all weighed on his shoulders. "Tuttle was a sick man. He kept Clara's body after Detective Castillo killed her. He wanted it as leverage against Hamonte—just in case he needed it."

It was all so much—so many secrets, lies and truths being revealed after 20 years.

Lincoln scoffed and stared at the ground. "I've been planning this for so long, you have no idea. The people I've killed...the things I've done, for Tuttle. That's why I finally killed him. You know what pushed me over the edge?"

I paused for a moment, not sure on what he was about to say. "What?"

"Tuttle sent me to kill Angela. That restoration project she was planning? She was looking too closely into things, into the funding for the institute. She would've caught on—so she needed to go. That was my opportunity. First, I killed Tuttle. He always saw me off when he sent me to execute people. That was his biggest mistake. Then I went to your house and took her—dragged her all the way here."

I staggered backwards, almost dropping the gun, an ice pick plunging through my heart. "What? She's...dead? She's dead?" I asked shakily, tears streaming down my eyes, my cheeks flushed. "Why? Why would you do that?" I sobbed quietly.

"I didn't kill her. She's still alive."

I had some relief from that statement, but not nearly enough, after everything I had gone through. "You've put me through so much hell, Lincoln. Where's Angela? Please. Where is she? She's innocent in all of this. Please!" I begged him.

He shook his head slowly. "No. I'm not done yet. You will understand why I've done all of this—to slowly destroy you. I wanted to mold *you* into a killer, just like how Tuttle molded me into one." He shut his eyes, tilting his head upward. "The way he forced me to do his bidding, he convinced me that he had saved me and that I owed him my life."

"How? How does that make any sense? This is all insane, Lincoln! Absolutely insane!"

He opened his eyes, bringing his head back down. "I played this game with you because Tuttle had played it with me. 25 days to execute. 12 gifts that related to the person I needed to kill for him. I decided to do the same, and put my own twist on it—just for you." He let out a dry laugh. "I knew how much you loved Angela because of Tuttle. Then it all came back to me—he reminded me of when you abandoned me, betrayed me...left me behind with a monster!" he shouted ferociously.

I breathed in deeply, not knowing what to say. I couldn't believe that my own brother had done this to me. He had forced me to become a killer, just like him.

I knew the outcome of his twisted game.

I had become the Xmas Day Butcher.

This is what he had wanted all along. This is what his long game of revenge led to. He forced me to become a killer.

I sighed, and stared at the ground, sick and tired of it all. My mind was a revolving door of dark thoughts—rooted in pain and misery.

This was a Christmas Day I would remember forever, for all of the wrong reasons.

"What must I do, to get Angela back? Please, you got what you wanted. I'm a killer now, like you. I'm the Xmas Day Butcher. Please...tell me what you want from me," I pleaded desperately.

He pointed at my gun. "Drop it and kick it over to me. If you try anything, Angela will die."

I immediately dropped it and kicked it over to him, I wasn't taking any chances. He picked it up and stuffed it in his back pocket. He grabbed something hanging near him, I hadn't noticed it before. It was a rope, tied to a beam up high.

"Stay here. I will bring her out. Don't you dare move."

I did as instructed, I didn't want him to hurt Angela. He walked away into darkness. It wasn't long before he took out Angela, his hands firmly on her dirty, white shirt. She was gaunt, with heavy dark circles around her eyes and she looked malnourished, but alive. My poor love. She was alive.

I was relieved to see that she had all of her limbs in tact. "Angela, oh my god! Angela!" I wanted to rush towards her, to hug her, kiss her, to hold her so tight and never let go. But Lincoln held up his hatchet at me and shook his head violently.

"No! Stay right there."

Angela glanced at me, fear in her eyes, and quickly averted her gaze. My poor wife—she had been held captive for 25 days. Lincoln had destroyed her, physically and mentally. I could never forgive him.

"Lincoln, please! Please! What now?! What must I do?! Please let her go! She has nothing to do with any of this!"

He ignored me and led my trembling wife to a broken pew—to stand on it. He grabbed the hanging rope, wrapped it around her neck and tightened it as I watched in shock, my heart nearly stopping at the sight of my terrified wife, death on her doorstep.

Lincoln swung the hatchet down into the church floorboards with a hard *crack*, splintering the wood. His bloodshot eyes found me.

"One choice, Lenny," he said. "Kill me, for everything I've done to you...or save her."

Angela was behind him, the rope cutting into her neck; her feet barely touching the top railing of the pew. She's sobbing quietly—utterly exhausted. My heart slammed against my ribcage.

A twisted grin formed on Lincoln's face. "Merry Christmas, brother. Choose wisely."

Before I could breathe, he gave Angela a gentle push and ran away, disappearing into the darkness. Angela lost her balance, hanging in the air and choking on the rope. "No!" I shouted.

I sprinted for the hatchet, fingers slipping on the handle as I yanked it free from the floorboards. I rushed to save Angela, hacking at the rope until it snapped. When it did she collapsed onto me, coughing and wheezing—attempting to catch her breath. I folded her into my arms, relief pouring through me. She was safe. She was alive. "Oh, my love. How I've missed you."

When she gathered herself she shoved me away violently. I stared at her, stunned. I didn't understand. Why was she acting like that? It was over. It was finally over.

"Angela?" I don't understand. "It's me. I found you. It's over."

She looked at me like I was a stranger. "I know what you did, Lenny. All those people...all the murders. Lincoln told me every-thing. You're a killer, Lenny."

My stomach dropped.

No. This can't be happening.

A chill ran down my spine as I feared the worst. "Angela, honey, I did it for you. To find you. To save you. You were gone...I had to do those things to save you."

"No." she shook her head, tears running down her face. "This is all your fault. Look what you've done to me. You're just like him. You're like your brother."

The words ripped into my body, tearing my insides to shreds. I had lost my wife. Lincoln had truly taken everything from me. He got his revenge. He destroyed me.

She backed away from me and reached behind her waistband. She pulled out a gun my brother had given her.

"He told me to use it on you, if I felt I needed to," she whispered. "He said...he said you're not my husband anymore. You're the Xmas Day Butcher."

She raised the gun at me, hands trembling. I lifted my palms and stepped slowly towards her.

"Angela, no. Listen to me. He's twisting everything. He's poisoned your mind. You were abducted for 25 days. Don't let him do this to us. Let me help you. I am your husband, and I love you." A sob broke out of me. "I did so much for you. I killed for you, Angela. Please, let's fix this."

She flicked the safety off, her eyes becoming cold and distant.

I saw something close inside her—something final. Our love...torn, ruined, destroyed by Lincoln's hands.

Angela sobbed, her shoulders shaking. "He kept me in a cold, dark place for 25 days...all because of you. He told me everything you've done. Nothing can ever be the same, ever again."

She fired the gun.

I fully expected to die in that moment. I closed my eyes, ready to accept my fate. If I didn't have Angela's love, what else was there?

But, I survived.

The shot whizzed past my ear, ricocheting off the wall. She had missed. She then dropped the gun, collapsing to her knees.

"I can't do it," she whispered, her voice cracking. "Lenny, I can't live with this. I can't live with any of it. Please...end it. End me."

After everything, this is how it ended with Angela. After everything I had done—all the people I had murdered in her name...it was over. She was right. We could never be the same, ever again. I was a killer.

After 25 days of hell, my life ended on an unforgiving Christmas Day.

"No." I knelt beside her, touching her cheek lightly. "Never. I love you. I always will. I swear I'll make him pay for what he did to us."

I stood up.

"If I'm a killer now...so be it. I am the Xmas Day Butcher, and my next victim is my brother—the Dollhouse Killer."

I grabbed the hatchet and the gun. I charged out into the cold darkness, winds howling in my ears. I promised myself I'd find Lincoln Frost. I'd make him pay for everything he had done to me—no matter how long it took.

The hunt had begun.

EPILOGUE

Lenny tried his best to hunt down Lincoln Frost, his twin brother, but he disappeared—like a ghost in the wind. He went into hiding, changing his name and his appearance.

He worked any construction jobs he could find—the ones that wouldn't ask for any identification, the ones that paid under the table. He lived in abandoned cars, underneath bridges, and occasionally he'd spend a few nights in a motel when he could spare the cash.

Eventually, he made his return to Whisper's Creek—several years later. But, under a new name—Lonnie Jacobs. A twisted serial killer hiding in plain sight. But his urges never vanished, and he looked forward to the day when he'd be able to strike again, as the *Dollhouse Killer*.

One thing he didn't know, however, was that the Xmas Day Butcher—the monster he had created, was close to finding him.

The hunt was on. One day, they would meet again.

10 YEARS LATER

A different kind of monster—a sinister, depraved man with a disturbing mind would abduct a young woman in Whisper's Creek.

The "Cycle" begins...

Read the twisted, unhinged thriller now: LOCKED IN A STRANGER'S ROOM.

It'll leave you gasping for air when you let out the breath you didn't know you were holding.

Don't say I didn't warn you...

THANK YOU READER!

Thank you so much for reading *THE XMAS DAY BUTCHER!* If you loved this book, be sure to stay subscribed to my newsletter for free books, updates about future books and more!

Visit https://www.spencerguerreroauthor.com to sign up!

Please consider leaving a review! I read them all! It helps me immensely as an author! Feel free to tag me as well:

My Socials:

Instagram: @SpencerGAuthor

Facebook: https://www.facebook.com/spencer.gue rrero.71

Facebook Readers Group: @THE SUSPENCERS

TikTok: @SpencerGAuthor

MORE BOOKS!

MY SON IS A MURDERER

MY FATHER IS A SERIAL KILLER

MY WIFE'S STALKER

A MURDER IN THE NEIGHBORHOOD

MY MOTHER-IN-LAW MUST DIE

THE NIGHT THEY TOOK MY SON

LOCKED IN A STRANGER'S ROOM

They're all available on paperback/digital formats on Amazon and Kindle Unlimited!

AUDIBLE TITLES:

MY SON IS A MURDERER

MY FATHER IS A SERIAL KILLER

MY WIFE'S STALKER

A MURDER IN THE NEIGHBORHOOD

MY MOTHER-IN-LAW MUST DIE

THE NIGHT THEY TOOK MY SON (December Release)

ACKNOWLEDGEMENTS

To my new and loyal readers, you are the lifeline. You are the reason I write books. You are the reason why I'm so passionate to get these stories out there. I'm very lucky to have you all. I read and appreciate every single review beyond measure. I love writing books and I love being able to share mine with you all!

A HUGE thank you to my Editor for helping me polish and improve these delightfully wicked stories.

A BIG thank you to all members of these Facebook Book Groups for your support! *Psychological Thriller Readers, Psychological Thrillers Book Club 2x, Linda and Friends Book Club, and Tattered Page Book Club.*

I also want to express my immense gratitude and thanks to my exemplary **ARC READERS** and **BETA READERS!** Thank you for always reading, reviewing, recommending, sharing and posting about my books! You guys are **AWESOME!**

SUSPENCERS BABY!

ABOUT THE AUTHOR

My name is Spencer Guerrero. I was born and raised in Florida, and I am of Nicaraguan descent. I am a self-published author and writer of psychological thrillers and mystery/suspense novels.

I used to be a freelance screenwriter and was hired to write a religious sci-fi/fantasy book adaptation, an animated Christmas film script, three short films and other work that included writing and outlining stories for licensed animated characters.

I decided to switch avenues so I could focus on the type of stories I wanted to write. Self-publishing looked like the best route, and I haven't looked back since.

My favorite genres are YA fiction, mystery-thriller, fantasy, and literary fiction. Other than that, I like funny cat memes, dark comedies and I play basketball!

Printed in Dunstable, United Kingdom

73961746R00118